Hair Calamities and Hot Cash

Gail Pallotta

Blessings,

Gail Pallotta

Hair Calamities and Hot Cash
COPYRIGHT 2018 by Gail Pallotta

Contact Information: titleadmin@pelicanbookgroup.com

All scripture quotations, unless otherwise indicated, are taken from the Holy Bible, New International Version[R], NIV[R], Copyright 1973, 1978, 1984, 2011 by Biblica, Inc.™ Used by permission of Zondervan. All rights reserved worldwide. www.zondervan.com

Cover Art by *Nicola Martinez*

Prism is a division of Pelican Ventures, LLC
www.pelicanbookgroup.com PO Box 1738 *Aztec, NM * 87410

The Triangle Prism logo is a trademark of Pelican Ventures, LLC

Publishing History
Prism Edition, 2018
Paperback Edition ISBN 978-1-5223-9791-5
Electronic Edition ISBN 978-1-5223-9790-8
Published in the United States of America

Dedication

For my mother, Evelyn Mathis Cassady.

Acknowledgements

Thank you to hairstylist Carlee Cowin and my writing partner, Lisa Lickel, for their encouragement and input; to my publisher, Nicola Martinez, and my editor, Jamie West, for believing in *Hair Calamities and Hot Cash*, and to God for His many blessings.

What People are Saying

A car crash, a threatening note, crazy hair? What is going on in Eve Castleberry's salon? She turns to handsome, stockbroker Philip Wells for help. What ensues is a comedic romp from small town to big city in search of missing money, hair catastrophes, and love. A truly fun read.

~Cynthia Hickey, author of
Shady Acres Mystery series

1

Philip Wells glanced at the majestic blue-tinted mountains in the distance. New York City stress fell from him like the waterfall he passed on his right. He turned into a winding curve and climbed a steep grade flush with green hardwoods, white dogwood blossoms, and pink wildflowers. His taut muscles loosened. If he'd known the Western North Carolina Mountains would bring such peace, he would've *asked* George to send him here on a business trip.

He'd resented leaving the country club when George appointed him to take care of Mr. Jacobsen's account, but not anymore. Riding through these hills gave him new-found freedom. His heart danced until he zipped into another curve at the edge of a cliff and glimpsed the precipice beyond the guard rail. He gripped the steering wheel as the need to secure his space on solid ground rushed through him.

He'd driven on the highway for miles and hadn't seen another car. According to the GPS, he'd round a few more bends and pull into Triville, located sixty miles northwest of Asheville. George had reserved a room for him at Triville Motel near the base of Mr. Jacobsen's mountain. Philip glanced at the towering peaks surrounding him and tried to imagine owning one. George had instructed him to contact Mr. Jacobsen, let him know he'd arrived, and set up a meeting.

Who would've thought Make More Money's newest and biggest client would live up here? Hey, he could see how the guy wanted to own one of these magnificent hills. He'd never seen a view this gorgeous out his office window, but what about the coffee houses, parties, custom-tailored suits, and civilization? What made someone tick who chose this type of life? Did the old codger not like people? A twinge of uneasiness pricked Philip's skin. What sales approach should he use?

Philip rounded a curve, and a truck barreled toward him on his side of the road. His heart jumped in his throat as he swerved to miss it. It grazed the side of Philip's car, jarring him while sending his vehicle onto the shoulder. Philip's heart clenched. He steered toward the road and tapped the brake as he started downhill, but his car gained speed. The trees blurred as he whizzed past them. He mashed the pedal. It slammed to the floorboard, and a helpless sensation rippled over Philip. His leg shook as he pumped again and again.

~*~

The bright May sun beaming through the window of my beauty shop created a stripe across the black shampoo bowl. Every day the ache in my heart for Jordan reminded me that Eve's Clips was my life now. I leaned Joyce Westmoreland's head back and scrubbed her blonde locks. Then I reached for the conditioner on the metal shelf behind the shampoo bowl. The bottle was empty, and it was the last one I had. That ne'er-do-well Durbin Brown hadn't delivered my products.

A breeze hit me in the face as the door swung open, the pink flowered curtain flapping.

"Hello, where have you been? You were supposed to come on Monday." I held out the container. "I'm out." My insides boiled at such bad service, not to mention that my creepy new salesman reminded me of Ichabod Crane.

He plopped down several cardboard boxes, ripped the top off one and handed me Strawberry Fields Conditioner.

"Thank you."

Durbin pulled a small pad out of his pants pocket, flipped it open, and tapped his foot. "I'm writing a bill for you."

The building shook. Metal crunched. Bricks fell amid loud scraping.

My nerves vibrated.

Durbin's mouth twitched.

Joyce bounded out of her chair.

"Quick, under the vanity," I yelled out.

Joyce shot to it like a bullet, but Durbin froze. I grabbed his spindly arm and pulled him behind me, the heels on his black boots scraping across the gray laminate floor. "Get under here." I couldn't help but use a harsh tone. He hunkered down, and I scooted in beside Joyce. He nuzzled into my shoulder and shivered like a wet puppy. My head spun as the walls shook, shards of glass fell, and drywall dust trickled into the air.

Finally, the structure stood still and quiet. I crawled out, and my legs nearly buckled under me.

Joyce and Durbin followed.

Then we all turned toward the window.

My heart sank and landed like a rock in my stomach.

A blue car stuck through the wall and lower portion of the large glass window. Two airbags filled the vehicle's cracked windshield.

I stumbled to a salon styling chair and dropped down. First Jordan, now this. Was the driver all right? Would the ladies of Triville desert me if I couldn't fix their hair?

Joyce plunked down in the chair in front of the shampoo bowl. She appeared shaken, water trailing down her face from the half-rinsed hair. Durbin was as white as Triville's winter snow, the smirk he usually wore gone. He collapsed in the seat underneath the upturned hair dryer as the door on the driver's side of the wrecked car creaked.

A man with a trim athletic build staggered out.

I swallowed my tears and stared at him. I'd never seen him before. As handsome as he was I'd remember if I had.

In moments he opened the shop door and joined us. "Ma'am, I'm sorry. Is everyone all right?"

My insides exploded with sorrow over my ruined shop, but I wasn't physically harmed. "I'm OK." I directed my gaze at Joyce.

"Just frightened," she said.

Durbin leapt up as though someone had injected him with adrenalin, stiffened, and held out his writing pad and pencil. "Back to your bill."

How could he think about that now? I must've looked at him as though he had three eyes, because he said, "I have other clients." He gestured toward the stranger with his pencil. "I can't stay here just because this dude rammed his car through the window. I have to keep moving."

"All right."

He pointed to a line on the small notebook, and I signed. "Would you please come on Monday next month?"

"It's out of my way, so I have to make a special trip, but I'll try. I suppose all the ladies need to spruce up for the Cow Flop Festival or whatever is on the busy agenda on the outskirts of nowhere." The familiar smirk reappeared.

Joyce clenched her jaw, sat up, and ruffled the burgundy cape I'd placed over her blouse. "Now, you wait just a minute, Mr. uh..."

Durbin brushed drywall dust from his lapel. "Brown, Durbin Brown."

I wanted to tell him to take his products and never come back, but I needed them, and my shop was at the base of a mountain quite a distance from most salesmen's routes. He turned and strutted out the door.

"I apologize for the mess I've made, but..." the man who'd run into my shop peered at me with pleading, powder-blue eyes. "I need to use your landline." He shook his cell phone. "This thing won't work."

If only Jordan were here. My head swirled as I tried to think what to do about Joyce's hair, keep my blood from boiling over at Durbin, and not cry over the disaster this man had made in my shop. The color had drained from the poor guy's face. *What did he say? Oh, his cell phone won't work.* "No, it wouldn't. Eve's Clips is in a dead zone."

The way he gazed at me he might as well have said, *I agree. This whole town's in a dead zone.*

Ralph Wisner and his wife lived in the house next

door, the only people for miles around. They both worked all day, or they would've been over here to see what was going on. Triville was a nosey place, but everyone knew everyone else, and people cared about each other.

"Uh..." I gestured toward the landline, sitting untouched on my desk. "Help yourself."

Joyce stared at the man with wide eyes.

"I'll need to cancel my appointments today, but I'll finish your hairdo." I tried to reassure Joyce then I re-directed my gaze to the man. "Sir, if you don't mind, sit at this end of the desk away from the debris." I tapped the unaffected area. We dared not touch anything until the police and insurance adjuster checked the damage.

"Yes, ma'am." He pulled out the straight-back chair with a flowered cushion that matched the curtains.

The glass crunched, and I shivered inside at the mess he'd made. What was he doing way out here? Eve's Clips was on the main highway, which wound up steep hills dotted with pines, hardwoods, and apple trees. Few people traveled it after November thirtieth when the tourists left.

Joyce touched her tresses. "I appreciate your willingness to fix my hair. I can't go to work like this."

The man spoke into the receiver. "Mr. Jacobsen, this is Philip Wells. I'm sorry, but I'll be late arriving at your house. I'm at Eve's Clips in Triville. I've had a bit of car trouble."

That was putting it mildly.

He kept his ear glued to the phone. "Yes sir, I appreciate your patience." The man's pale, handsome face drooped.

It wouldn't hurt me to show him and Joyce some southern hospitality. "We need to call the police." I looked at the man. "And your insurance adjuster. But why don't I go in the house and bring us all a cup of coffee?" I stuck out my hand. "I'm Eve Castleberry." I motioned toward Joyce. "Joyce Westmoreland."

Joyce gave a half-smile.

He shook my hand. "Philip Wells. I'm sorry to meet under these circumstances. I phoned my insurance company before I called Mr. Jacobsen, but as for the police, should I contact 911?"

"No, call the sheriff, Thad Waters. I'm on the outskirts of town." My shivering nerves calmed a bit knowing he understood his responsibility. I went to my desk and turned on the laptop. Shards of glass hit the floor, and the urge to slap the stranger for ruining my shop hit me like a lightning bolt, but he peered at me with regret-filled blue eyes that soothed my anger.

"That's Thad's number." I pointed to it on the screen. "Thad grew up here. He's so mild-mannered it's hard to imagine him running down criminals. However, at six-feet-three inches he's big enough to intimidate most people, and he's wanted to be a sheriff for as long as I can remember. He'll assess this situation accurately." Words flowed from my mouth as though they had been programmed.

"He sounds like the person we need. How about a tow truck?"

"Call Lloyd Rock. His number's there too." I took a step back and tried to grasp how the wreck happened. "What went wrong?"

"My brakes failed." The man slumped in the chair.

"I see." I understood his words, but the disaster in my shop still seemed surreal. "Well, I'll be right back."

I patted Joyce on the knee. "Don't worry. I'll have you as cute as a ladybug in no time after we have our coffee."

She flashed a forced-looking smile.

I left and went across the yard to the house, but the image of the car stuck in my window spun in my head. I unlocked the beveled glass door to tomb-like silence.

My coffee didn't taste as good as Jordan's. I missed the smell of the mocha blend wafting down the hall when I woke up. Most widows were middle-aged, and here I was only thirty-four. I'd never dated anyone but Jordan. Even if I had the will to try, most of the men in Triville were married. Tears rushed to my eyes.

If Jordan were here, he'd tell me everything would be fine, and I'd believe him. How long would repairs take? Would I have enough money to pay my bills this month? Would I find the will to get out of bed without an appointment?

I blinked back the tears as I passed the pine table and poured three cups of coffee from the pot I'd made this morning. I stuck them in the microwave with a shaky hand and tapped my foot while I waited. Finally, I set the mugs on a tray and headed toward the shop. I could at least style Joyce's hair and send her to work looking great, couldn't I? I pushed the door open with my shoe.

Joyce wiped dripping wet hair from her face, took two cups off the tray and handed one to the stranger. Then she sat back down in the shampoo chair and sipped.

I sank into a seat, swallowed, and welcomed the quiet filling my pores. Every bone in my body wanted to fix the shop immediately, but I needed to concentrate on giving Joyce a nice do. I got up, set her cup on the shelf above the shampoo bowl, and washed her hair, my eyes misting the entire time.

I applied the conditioner and suds built in the bowl. As upset as I was, maybe I'd picked up the shampoo. I turned up the product and stared at it—Strawberry Fields Conditioner. My stomach tightened as I ran my hands over her locks trying to work more water through them. The soap persisted, and my lower lip quivered.

2

The shampoo bowl faded as I stiffened my jaw and focused only on the suds stuck to Joyce's blonde hair. "My new salesman's products are different from those I've used in the past."

She peered at me with kind eyes. "I'm not worried, darlin.' I always look better when I leave here. Everyone knows you're the best hairstylist for miles around."

"Why thank you." I'd attended three refresher courses and salon shows to keep up with the latest trends. With all the strength left inside me, I wanted to work magic on Joyce's hair. I raised her up and patted her shoulder.

Foam from the shampoo bowl crept onto the floor. Her blue eyes widened. She tip-toed over the bubbles and plopped down in front of the mirror. As I worked I took a step to the right, slid, and gasped. From then on I snatched the curlers and rolled them in fast-forward speed. Could I produce a great hairstyle for Joyce amid this chaos? I showed her to the hair dryer, turned on the timer, and handed her a women's magazine.

The boxes Durbin had left soaked up the liquid oozing across the floor. I wanted to shake him, but he wasn't here. I glanced at the car in the window, and wanted to sit down and cry.

"Lloyd and Thad are on their way as well as the

insurance adjuster." Philip stood, and his gaze went to the floor then met mine. "What happened? You must use lots of shampoo."

"I put conditioner on Joyce's hair, and soap overflowed." I blinked back tears as I surveyed the disaster.

"I can't help you there. I don't know much about women's beauty supplies, but could I do something with those?" He pointed at the boxes.

I swallowed hard. "If you wouldn't mind."

"Of course, not, that's the least I can do. I'll unpack them too."

The heavy weight on my shoulders lightened. If he took care of that task, I could put away the clean towels and organize my supplies. "All right, thank you."

"Where would you like these?" He wrapped one arm around each container.

"I'll show you."

He followed me to the back of the shop and set the boxes on the floor. "What next?"

My supply closet was five boards installed above a chest, washer, and dryer in the narrow hall outside the restroom. "Just place the products right here." I patted an empty shelf.

Cardboard ripping filled the air as I folded towels. I stuffed some of them in a drawer in the chest then darted up front and laid a few on the shelf over the shampoo bowl. Concentrating on the small act of normalcy relaxed my tight muscles. If only I could close my eyes, open them, and see this was a bad dream. But it wasn't. Eve's Clips wouldn't be operational again soon.

The man returned to the front with a mop and

stared at the foam. "I don't mind cleaning up."

"No, that's all right, I'll get it la..."

The man's lips turned up on the corners, his gaze going soft and twinkly.

I smoothed my hair as warmth ran through my veins. That hadn't happened since my dear Jordan died. A pain pricked my heart because he was no longer with me, but I still had what was left of my shop. I grabbed at the mop. "Here, I'll take that."

"No. I'm happy to help." He stopped the creeping bubbles before they flowed into the glass shards. I sighed in relief.

The foaming mess inched up on his pants.

"Oh, no. Your expensive clothes are ruined." I bent down and brushed his trouser legs off. "I'll bring a hair blower right now."

Philip stood in the soapsuds, gazing at his leather slip-on shoes with tassels across the tops. "You have a point. Well, all right, we can dry them."

What was he thinking traipsing around in the middle of that watery disaster wearing his good clothes? I dried the slacks then smoothed them with my hand. "If they shrank it's not enough to tell. They look fine."

"Sure, it's nothing to worry about. I'll sit over here and wait for Mr. Rock." He took a few steps, and the liquid seeped from his socks over the sides of his shoes. He snatched a towel off the shelf behind the shampoo bowl and wiped it. His lips turned up on the corners in a sheepish grin as though he now realized he may have ruined his fancy loafers. He looked like a little kid who'd gotten the last cookie out of the jar.

The timer buzzed.

Joyce lifted the dryer off her head, moved to the

second hairstylist chair and sank into it.

I placed my hand near her scalp to avoid yanking out strands of hair as I struggled to untangle it. She said nothing, and my pulse quickened at her silence. Did she expect me to fashion my usual beautiful "do" out of the twisted, snarls?

She sneezed as I applied more gel. "I hope you aren't allergic to drywall dust. I'm sorry." I glimpsed at the hood of the car in the window and nearly gagged.

"It's all right. I'm fine."

I combed so much gel through her hairdo it wilted like the camellia blossoms right before they fell off the bush. Her creased brow reflected onto the mirror, and my heart sank. I parted off sections of her hair, grabbed the curling iron and created ringlets. I brushed them out, and they crimped as if she'd stuck her finger in a live electrical socket. I covered my mouth to conceal my gasp. My reputation, my livelihood, all that I lived for frizzed out of control.

Joyce whipped off the burgundy cape and bounded out of the chair. "I have to hurry home. Hubby will be worried." Her eyes glistened. She was too kind to say anything rude.

My self-confidence shrank to nothing. "I'm sorry your hair's unruly. If you'll come back, I'll style it for free."

"Maybe I can do something with it at the house. I hope it won't look like this tomorrow when I go to work."

The sole person in charge of customer service at Ray's Department Store on Main Street, Joyce handled exchanges and wrapped gifts for customers. I doubted she wanted to face them with her hair out of control.

The stranger had his chin lowered as though he

tried to hide a large smile. Joyce patted her locks. "Could you wet it? Maybe it'll have less volume." She sat down in front of the shampoo bowl.

My hands froze. Did I dare? I had to. I thoroughly drenched Joyce's tresses then towel-dried them.

She marched out with wet, unmanageable hair. Would mine and Joyce's friendship go down the drain with a bottle of conditioner? Would she drive to the big beauty shop chain in Misty Gorge from now on? Would all of my customers go there? I plopped down in the shampoo chair and slumped as a dull pain hit me in the chest.

Philip stared at the car, the spring breeze blowing what was left of the curtains. "I hope you won't have to use that product again."

I forced words over the knot in my throat. "I won't for a while. Tomorrow night is the Spring Gala for the ninth and tenth graders at Triville High and prom for the Juniors and Seniors. I'm booked all day with dry haircuts and up-dos for the girls and clips for the boys. Each year as my gift to the students, I let them wash their hair then come in. I charge only a small fee. Each of them won't be here long, and the kids won't mind the mess."

Suddenly Philip's eyes lit up as though something had encouraged him.

The door opened, and Lloyd entered. He'd studied automobile mechanics at a small community college and knew more about cars than anyone I'd ever met. Knowing he'd remove the monster from my window sent a tingle of hope rippling over my skin. He shook his head. "Hmm, hmm, I'm sorry, Eve." He cast his gaze at Philip. "I've assessed this situation. I'll be back to tow the car after the insurance adjuster leaves. Me and my assistant, Lou, will bring you a rental about four o'clock as soon as Miss Millie turns in one of them."

"All right." Resignation lined Philip's voice.

Lloyd's hairstyle was out of shape.

"We need to make an appointment for you."

Lloyd touched the shaggy hairdo. "I know. I'll call." He left, and an awkward silence fell.

I tried not to look at the disaster, but I couldn't help it. "When did you say the insurance adjuster is coming?"

"No later than two-thirty or three."

"I need to use the phone to call my customers."

"Yes, ma'am, I'm sorry. I didn't mean to take over the clean end of your desk."

If only that was all he'd done. He'd ruined my income and my social life. Since Jordan died only my customers connected me to the small town outside my beauty shop. "It's all right."

Hoping not to disturb any more debris at the other end, I inched the drawer open and snatched my appointment book. Just today I'd have to cancel slots for eight people. My hands shook as I turned to the first page, but I persisted until I contacted everyone scheduled for this afternoon and received their sympathies for the mishap.

Philip looked like a beaten pup.

He *was* in a strange town where he knew no one and he'd had an accident. I should at least make conversation. "Where are you from, if you don't mind my asking?"

~*~

15

Not only did Philip not mind Eve asking, relief that she'd talk to him soothed his ragged nerves. "Of course not, I'm from New York City. I work for Make More Money."

Eve nearly knocked the laptop off the desk. "Make More Money with the ad on television that says, 'Make more money with us?" She peered at Philip with dark, wide eyes.

He swallowed his chuckle. "That's the one."

"And you're here to see Mr. Jacobsen. He lives about fifty miles away. Sold a lot of his land to some casino people from Las Vegas. We voted not to allow them here, but Mr. Jacobsen has so much property. They can plant themselves on his mountain and do whatever they want. They won't bother us down here a bit. We might see an increase in traffic. That's all."

Philip welcomed any information about Mr. Jacobsen, but an awful itch on his leg distracted him. He couldn't resist leaning down to scratch it.

"Probably dried soap from all that sudsy water you mopped up for me. I'm sorry."

"No, it's fine." Philip noticed a piece of paper beside his foot. He picked it up and handed it to Eve. "This has your name on it."

Eve grasped it.

"It must have fallen off your desk in the crash and blown over here."

"No. Only the appointment book was out." She studied it and the color drained from her face.

Philip sprang from his seat and guided her to a salon chair. "Are you OK? What does it say?"

Eve handed it to him.

"Do you know anyone who wants to hurt you?"

"No, but a week ago I read an article in the *Merchantville News* about businesses that received threatening notes. A few days afterward they were robbed. This relates to my beauty shop." Eve's breath hitched.

"Did they catch the thief?"

"No. What if he expanded his territory?" Eve blinked as though she fought tears.

Philip yearned to comfort her. "It never hurts to be careful, but try not to worry." He pondered the note. "Do you have youngsters in here?"

Eve tilted her head. "Sure, they come with their parents."

"It's probably a kid. No adult would write, 'You're going to be a DIE-ed blond soon." Philip tried to sound convincing.

"You're right. I'm overreacting...the wreck, and all." Her voice held less strain.

"That's understandable."

Sheriff Thad entered, removed his brown felt hat, and ran his hand through dark hair. "Hello, Eve." Worry lined his voice as he directed his gaze at Philip. "Are either of you hurt?"

"No." Philip gave a silent prayer of thankfulness.

Thad nodded. "Good, but call a doctor and let him know what's happened. If anything shows up later, he'll have an accident report on file."

"Thanks, I'll do that."

"All right, give me a blow by blow." Thad whipped a pad out of his pants pocket.

"I was riding along then all of a sudden a logging truck flew down the road and headed straight at me. I swerved, but he grazed the side of the rental car as I started down the incline. I put on my brakes, but they didn't work. I pumped the pedal, but the rental car kept speeding until I crashed into the wall." Philip swung his arm toward the window. "You can see the rest."

"Where's the driver of the other vehicle?"

"I have no idea."

"So he didn't stop. Do you remember anything about the truck?"

"I only saw it for a second. Any longer and I'd have been in it, but let me think." Philip rubbed his forehead. "Ahh, yeah, it had a black cab and a flatbed loaded with logs."

"I'll put out an all-points bulletin for loggers for the entire surrounding area." Thad pulled his eyebrows together. "I hate to say this, but in addition to reckless driving, he might not have insurance. That's probably the reason he left the scene of the accident."

"I know." Resignation rang in Philip's voice.

"Sorry." Thad headed out the door then looked over his shoulder. "See you later, Eve."

What if George had tried to contact him? An uneasy sensation pulsed through Philip's veins. "Do you mind if I use your computer to check e-mail?"

"Of course not."

He plunked down at Eve's desk.

A lanky man entered the shop. "Hello, ma'am, I'm Gregg Roberts with Count-on-Us Insurance."

"Come in." Eve's voice sounded weak.

Within fifteen minutes Mr. Roberts had recorded Eve's needs for the wall, window, and a small crack in the ceiling. "We've arranged for workers to arrive this afternoon and secure the window as soon as Mr. Rock tows the car." He handed a card to Eve and one to Philip. "I'm almost finished. I'll snap a few pictures outside and be on my way."

Philip glanced at Eve. She seemed all right, but the sooner Lloyd removed the car the better.

Lloyd must have been on Mr. Roberts's heels. He stuck his head in the door and directed his gaze toward Philip. "I'll pull out the vehicle, but Miss Millie hasn't turned in the rent-a-car. Me and Lou will be over here with it as soon as she does."

Joy sparked through Philip. He couldn't wait to slip into the seat of a car, slide his hand around the steering wheel and know he was no longer stranded, even though he had to admit he'd enjoyed getting to know Eve. "I understand. I'll see you then."

Lloyd ducked outside. In moments a roar penetrated the room and the wall shook.

Eve trembled.

Philip wanted to hold her. "I'm so sorry. I wouldn't have ruined your shop for the world if I could've..."

"I know."

The building stilled, and a huge cavity appeared. Eve turned as white as the drywall dust and sank down in a hairstylist chair, her eyes misty. Guilt eked into Philip. If only he could make it up to her.

Two workmen with blond hair and blue eyes who could've passed for twins burst through the doorway.

Eve shot out of the chair. "Hi Pete, Charlie, I'm so glad you're here."

Pete stared at the gaping hole. "It looks as though we arrived just in time." He put his hand on the hammer stuck in his brown leather belt.

Eve glanced at Philip. "Philip Wells, meet Triville's best handymen." A hint of hope filled Eve's voice. Philip shook hands with the guys as she added,

"Pete and Charlie have loved building for as long as I can remember. They even won awards for some of their projects when we were in high school."

Pete and Charlie grinned.

"Ahh, we're just carpenters," Charlie said.

"We'll clean and patch the hole." Pete peered at Eve. "Try not to worry. It'll look great when we finish."

The two of them left and returned carrying a broom, mop, and large metal dust pan. They dispensed with the debris and placed heavy plastic over the gaping void. "We'll pick up your replacement window unit at Builder's Supply in Misty Gorge and install it as quickly as possible," Pete said.

"Thanks, guys."

They left, and Philip plunked down at Eve's desk. "I'm sorry about all of this."

"I know you are." Eve tapped the threatening message she'd laid on top of her appointment book. "I should've asked Thad what he thought about the note."

All of the tenderness Philip had in him reached out to Eve. "It probably was a kid, but you could call Thad."

"No, I'm sure you're right."

"I see Lloyd and Lou outside. I've made such a mess of your shop. Please let me take you to dinner. It's the least I can do." Philip held his breath waiting for Eve's answer.

"There's no need. I should thank you for helping me mop."

"If you join me I won't have to eat alone. That's enough."

~*~

For the first time in a long time I wouldn't nibble a one-dish microwaveable meal with no one to talk to. Could I go out with any man other than Jordan? My heart flip-flopped. Six months ago I couldn't have done it, but something about this guy attracted me. Had Philip triggered a yearning for companionship I didn't know I had? He was only passing through town. It was just a meal. "We could meet at Bob's Diner. What time do you want to go?"

"Seven o'clock, if that's OK."

"Perfect."

"See you in an hour at Bob's Diner."

Philip left and I headed outside. What an unsettling, ironic day it'd been in my quiet little beauty shop where nothing ever interrupted my hum-drum life. I locked up, crossed the patch of grassy yard to my cement porch, and opened the door to the house. And then it hit me. I had a date.

The anticipation of seeing Philip for dinner sent happiness surging through me. He awakened a light-heartedness I hadn't known since Jordan died. I couldn't help but snicker as I danced across the beige carpet to the walk-in closet in the bedroom. A widow courting and feeling like a teenager. Of course, this wasn't a real date. It was a thank you dinner. What to wear?

There was the new, dark brown dress I purchased two weeks ago on impulse. Then I'd thought how silly and wasteful to buy something for a special occasion. I didn't have those anymore. I'd never wear it.

I held it next to my chest. Was it meant for this evening?

3

Gravel crunched as I parked in an empty space next to the white brick and metal building. The smell of French fries and hamburgers wafted outside, where a crowd gathered underneath the white and red awning. Modern restaurants resembled Bob's with its 1950's look, but a 1957 construction date gave his authenticity. Joyce stood four people in front of me with a kerchief over her hair. "Hi, Eve."

"Hey, how's it goin?'"

She touched the top of her head. "I'm working on it."

I shrank in guilt as Lloyd turned around.

He'd changed from his work clothes into a pair of jeans and a light blue shirt. "Hungry, Eve?"

"You bet."

"Things getting cleaned up in the shop?"

"Slowly, but surely."

He gave me a thumbs up.

The crowd moved forward, and I craned my neck as I entered. Where was Philip? What if he didn't show? I'd be the fool who tried to grab a brief moment of romance that didn't exist.

Ellie Ringgold waved from a booth with blue vinyl seats near the back beside a window. She was bold, robust, and good-hearted. She'd spent her life in Triville working in her father's furniture factory as a sales clerk and bookkeeper. After so many years of talking to customers, she could go anywhere, and chat with anybody. "Eve, hon, we heard about the excitement over at your place. You wanna' join us?"

She sat with her boyfriend, Smitty. He was the new love of her life. Her ex-husband used her to pay his way through dental school then left. Smitty didn't need her money. He owned the drugstore and a meat processing plant. He'd never married, but he'd had his sights set on Ellie since high school. He wasn't a handsome man with his squared jaw and oversized nose, but once a person knew his kind heart he looked a lot better.

"No thanks, I'm meeting someone."

The line moved quickly as people scooted into booths or plopped down at the counter.

"Looks like you're the only one waiting." Ellie pointed over her shoulder. "Folks right behind us just left. It's nice and cozy."

The insinuation in Ellie's voice reminded me of how little happened in Triville and how fast news spread when something did. Philip and I would be the talk of the town for at least a week. I slapped myself on the cheek as I plunked down in the seat. I didn't care. Philip stirred warmth that overshadowed the loneliness and sorrow inside me.

He breezed through the doorway, waved, and zigzagged around several chairs to reach me. "I'm sorry I'm late. I was delayed at the garage." Grinning, he took the seat across from me. "Lloyd's ordering a part for the car. No telling how long it'll take." Joy rang in his tone.

"Sounds as if you're stuck here for a day or so." I smiled as happiness erupted inside me.

"Longer. Mr. Jacobsen's visiting his daughter in Arkansas. My boss, George, wants me to stay put until he returns. Mr. Jacobsen will call your shop when he gets back."

"Why?"

"For some reason, my cell phone doesn't work in this area. He has your number because I called from Eve's Clips. What could I say?" Philip searched my face. "I thought it'd be OK. I hope it won't inconvenience you." Philip's voice sounded jittery.

"It's fine."

"I've checked out the sights and entertainment. Since I'll be here a while..." He grinned big "...and you probably need a distraction from the repairs, let's attend the piano concert tomorrow night on Blue Mountain."

Was he looking forward to another evening with me, or was he bored? Taking a message was one thing. Toying with my heart, another. What if going out with him again sent my already fragile emotions into a tailspin? I just met him, but it wasn't as if I were going out with a stranger. I'd spent an entire day in a crisis with Philip. We were friends. I gave him my best smile. "OK."

He picked up the menus from behind the mustard and ketchup bottles and handed me one. "What's good in here?"

"Chili cheeseburgers."

Bonnie Sue sashayed over to take our orders. She stuck her hand on her hip then cut her gaze at me. "Why, hello, Eve. This must be the handsome guy that nearly got killed at your shop?"

Bonnie Sue had green eyes with long lashes. Her auburn hair looked soft and touchable, the tips of it lying on the shoulders of her white uniform. The more men she went out with, the better she liked it. Her poor unsettled heart.

"Philip Wells, this is Bonnie Sue Jeffers."

"Nice to meet you."

Bonnie Sue sidled over to Philip and stood so close her side touched his shoulder. "What can I get for you, good lookin'?" She winked.

Heat crawled over my skin. Why should I care if Bonnie Sue flirted with Philip? Had this crazy day with its mix of disaster and newfound romance made me a little nuts?

He scooted away from the edge of the seat.

I couldn't control my satisfied smile.

"I'll have a chili cheeseburger and..." He peered at me. "What to drink?"

"Sweet tea, definitely. I'd like a chili cheeseburger too."

Bonnie Sue left as Lloyd pushed off his bar stool and ambled to our table.

Philip stood and shook his hand, but Lloyd peered at me.

"Why, I didn't know you were a friend of Eve's. I thought you got stranded in the shop."

Lloyd had no idea how I'd warmed up to a total stranger, but the earnest look in his eyes told me he wanted to correct his oversight. I fiddled with a napkin. "Ahh, that's right. We met today."

"Any friend of Eve's gets to use the Fix 'Em and Loan 'Em Garage and Car Rental freebie. Yes, siree. You bring that coupe back to me in the morning, and there won't be any charge."

"That's awfully nice of you, Mr. Rock, but I..."

There was no need for Philip to protest. Once

Lloyd made up his mind about something, it was as good as done.

"Not a 'tall. We take care of each other here in Triville. Ya'll enjoy yer dinner now, ya' hear."

Lloyd left and Philip shook his head. "I've never seen a place like Triville."

It had never occurred to me to compare Triville to another place, or its residents to other people, but Philip was different, more sophisticated and worldly. I could see him smooth talking his way into that ad on television about *Make More Money*, and I didn't understand why they hadn't used him.

Bonnie Sue served our food, grinning at Philip and leaning way over when she set down his cheeseburger. "I hope you like every little bite of that."

Philip scooted even farther away from the edge of the booth. "Thank you. I'm sure I will."

Obviously, he wasn't interested in her. I liked him even more.

He bit into his entree and his eyebrows shot up. He swallowed and held out the burger. "This is delicious."

Customers jammed into the diner, their chatter filling the room. A man in the booth across from us put a quarter in the small juke box on his table, and a fifties tune blasted from it.

I speared a French fry. "The potatoes are nice and crisp here." My voice faded into the sound of people talking and the music.

Philip leaned forward. "What?"

My words were babble. I hadn't been out with a man in so long I didn't know what to say. Heat built up and spread to my neck. "It wasn't important." I spoke loud without screaming.

We stopped trying to chat.

My embarrassment over my lack of dating faded, and we finished eating.

Philip trod to the front to pay, but returned and placed a five-dollar tip on the table. Such a generous gratuity would probably convince Bonnie Sue he was in love with her.

We wandered outside and stood underneath the soft glow of lighting in the parking lot.

"Can we go somewhere else? It was too noisy to talk in there." Philip's gaze moved along my face, his eyes pleading.

I wanted to spend more time with this mysterious, handsome man I barely knew. A voice in my head told me getting involved with someone simply passing through town was like attaching a bomb to my already wounded heart. Yet, how much of it could I really give him? He'd only stay long enough to see Mr. Jacobsen. When he left my infatuation would fly away with the mountain breeze. I had nothing to lose. "I suppose we could sit in the park across the street."

He clasped my hand, and in my heart I skipped along like a kid, warmth surging through my veins. We sat on a bench facing the blue-tinted mountains that isolated and shielded Triville from the outside world. Veiled in night's shadows, they towered around us. Occasional spotlights or a porch light cut into the dark halfway up one of them signaling signs of life.

The gentle wind that cooled Triville's evenings blew across my face as children behind us chattered, the swings squeaking. "Exactly what brings you to these hills to see Mr. Jacobsen? You seemed pretty upset this morning when you had to phone him because of the accident."

"Yeah. I was. Mr. Jacobsen wants to talk to someone from Make More Money in person about investing. He doesn't own a computer because he doesn't want anyone in cyber space snooping into his business. Phone conversations won't work either. He has a land line and a cell phone, but doesn't discuss business over either of them. He's only available face to face. That's why it's so important for me to be here when he returns."

"From what I hear about him, he's reclusive, but kind."

Philip nodded. "I'd say so, but I didn't realize that this morning. I thought I'd lost the account because I couldn't travel to his house. Between that and the car crash, I have to admit I was stressed out. You'll probably never believe it, but they call me *cool head* at work because I'm never rattled."

I chuckled, but I could see that. Philip seemed like a guy who had lived a life that groomed him to say and do the most appropriate thing in any situation, definitely a cool character. "If I'd known, I could've gotten a picture of you anxiously making those calls and sent it to them."

"You're bad." Philip planted a light tap on my arm.

"I don't believe you even heard me when I asked if you wanted coffee."

"Ahh, I have a one-track mind, especially in a disaster. I concentrate too intensely searching for a solution." Philip locked gazes with me. "I appreciated your kindness today. I think the people coming in the shop did too. It's interesting the way they're all so connected to you."

I burst out laughing. "It's not just me. All of

Triville's connected. We help each other out, but we know each other's business. It's easier to hold onto a greased pig than keep a secret in Triville. That's how I know Mr. Jacobsen sometimes visits Mary Louise as long as a month."

Philip's lips turned up on the corners. "So far, other than the wreck, it's a fun place. I could stay a month. I might have to check with George, but I'd like to hang out in Triville."

My heart fluttered. Was he saying he wanted to spend time with me? More importantly, why did I care? Confusion cluttered my mind, and sweat popped out on my forehead. I swiped my brow.

"George sends me out of town quite a bit to assess branch offices, hold seminars, or meet new clients, so he could easily pay a lot more for a hotel room somewhere else."

I nodded in agreement, but the excitement of being out with the second man I'd ever dated in my life plus the stress of the day caught up with me. My energy wilted like curled hair straightening in heavy dew. "I hate to leave, but a good night's sleep will help me tomorrow when I start on the cuts and up-dos."

"I'll swing by your place around six o'clock."

"Sounds good." The words popped out of my mouth as though I was under a spell. Had I adopted a new philosophy? One date at a time with no thought for tomorrow. I couldn't deny Philip tugged at my heart as no one had since Jordan. I shrugged my shoulders. Not much could happen in only a month, could it?

4

I stood barefoot on the beige carpet in the walk-in closet underneath the faint yellow glow of the small light. The school girls going to prom had nothing on me. I tingled with excitement as I dressed in a black skirt and jeweled knit shirt and twirled in front of the mirror. The doorbell rang, and I made tracks down the hall and answered.

Philip pushed back a lock of black hair falling over his forehead and smiled. "You look gorgeous." He leaned over, picked up a piece of paper, and handed it to me.

You could be in for a permanent sleep.

I'd convinced myself a bored kid wrote the first note. "Is someone threatening to...not again." I shook inside.

This wasn't a youngster's message to no one.

Furrows creased Philip's brow as he leaned over and peered at it. "I'm sorry I found it, but look. It has the same childlike lettering. It must've blown from the shop into the yard." He put his arm around my waist. "Don't worry. I believe it was the same boy or girl with nothing to do who penned the first one."

My jitters melted at his touch and reassuring words, and he guided me out. *Oh, no.* Lloyd's ornery 1965 classic. Why didn't he send Philip his newer loaner? I glanced at my coupe, but would it insult Philip if I suggested we take it?

He already held the passenger door open, gesturing toward the seat as though it was Cinderella's carriage. "Lloyd knows how to treat his customers. He refuses to charge me for this snazzy, black loaner vehicle." Philip's lips curved up. He eased into the driver's seat and backed out. "I don't have a map to Blue Mountain. Can you navigate?"

Finding the place wasn't the problem. "Sure. Who's playing tonight?"

"Jeffrey Combs, a music major from Western Hills College."

A classy evening. My heart swelled with pride for my little mountain community. Philip would see hillbillies weren't only about Uncle Fudd and Bubba pickin' and grinin.' Strange. Why would I care what he thought?

We rode through town past the shops and brick business offices, including Triville State Insurance Company, our tallest building at four stories. We started up the steep hill lined with oak and poplar trees when the classic car sputtered and bounced. I flew forward, braced myself when my hands hit the black vinyl dashboard, and looked at Philip. He'd probably never driven a car like this.

His eyes widened as he gripped the steering wheel so tight his knuckles turned white. *Poor guy.* "Are you all right?"

"I'm fine. I've ridden in this contraption before. It moves along on a level street. We could go back and eat in town."

"Oh, no. The Blue Room sounds nice." The vehicle surged and stalled. Philip floored the gas pedal. "How much farther? The last thing I need is another accident." He clenched his jaw.

Lloyd's "freebie" was enough to make an auto mechanic nervous on a steep grade. The trees and foliage looked pretty much the same no matter where we drove on the road. But spotlights on the house on the route lit up the night, and I knew its location. "We're a little over halfway there." Wanting to encourage him, I tried to sound upbeat.

"Good."

What could I say to make this trip easier, give him something besides the near stops of the old muscle car to think about? "How'd you become a stockbroker?"

"My dad used to discuss stocks and bonds so often Wall Street permeated my dreams. When I graduated from college, I landed the job in New York City with Make More Money."

The car popped and crept as though it might die any second. Philip pressed his lips tight, squared his jaw, and floor-boarded it. The car lunged forward.

I took a deep breath of relief. Philip was kind, and I suspected from his fine suit and expensive shoes, he was out of his culture zone. Driving the old car must've seemed awkward to him, but it appeared he intended to make the best of it. "It's great you snagged the position you wanted and can enjoy the city. I'd never fit in there."

Philip cut those sexy eyes toward me. "With your personality you could connect with anyone anywhere."

I sucked in air and exhaled slowly to anchor myself to the car seat as my head floated toward the clouds.

He kept talking as though he had no idea he'd sent me reeling. "I'm interested in moving to Narragansett Bay in Rhode Island. George says he'll consider letting me open a branch office there if I sign up Mr.

Jacobsen."

"Mr. Jacobsen's that important?" If he were, Philip might come back here to call on him. *Silly me.*

"Yeah, he's promised us a large investment and says he may increase it. His account would give our firm the boost it needs to expand."

"Make More Money already seems like a large company." Philip must have been awfully smart if Mr. Jacobsen's business meant that much and they chose him to handle the account.

The car sputtered, bumped ahead and then ran smoothly.

Philip loosened his grip on the steering wheel. "Hmm. This incline is leveling out. I guess we'll be OK now. What? Oh, yes, it's nice-sized, but a brokerage firm, or any other company, for that matter, can't have too much business."

"Right." I removed my hands from the dashboard as he pulled into a gravel lot on top of the mountain and parked in front of a tan stucco castle with a red roof.

Patrons in long dresses and fine suits emerged from luxury vehicles and sports cars as Philip slipped out and opened my door. A loud squeak pierced the night.

I gasped.

He flinched then looked at me, and we laughed.

In moments we entered a large room with a wall of screened casements. I couldn't help but notice the hostess's nicely-done French twist as she led us to a white, linen-draped table facing a baby grand piano.

A cool breeze from an opened window blew across my face, and my shoulders relaxed. Peace and contentment replaced the boredom and sorrow that had nagged me like a headache ever since Jordan died.

"It was worth the trip." Philip pulled up a tan captain's chair and sat back as a waiter appeared.

"How about spinach dip and two sweet teas?" Philip glanced at me.

"Sounds good." I'd forgotten how going out lifted my spirits. Until this moment, it hadn't occurred to me that I needed to take a break from the shop and enjoy a change of scenery. Did a nice looking guy have to ram his car through the wall of Eve's Clips for me to see that?

The waiter nodded and returned with the order as the pianist took the stage and bowed.

"The baby grand is made from spruce trees that grew on these mountains." I leaned forward and whispered to Philip.

"Very nice."

Jeffrey flipped up the tails on his black tuxedo and sat down. The room grew quiet, and the scrape of the bench echoed as he pulled it up. He placed his long fingers on the keyboard and opened with Tchaikovsky's Piano Concerto Number One.

The romantic melody and flickering candlelight sending soft hues across Philip's finely chiseled features whisked me to a field of daisies touched by sweet sunlight where lovers met and dreams came true.

The classical music ended and a round of loud applause erupted from the audience.

Jeffrey took another bow then resituated himself. The soothing notes of a Ferrante and Teicher tune wafted through the room.

Philip's eyes glinted with fascination.

Jeffrey concluded the first part of the concert with

Debussy's Clair de Lune then stood sporting a wide grin. "Thank you. I'll take a brief intermission, but don't go away."

Chatter and the sound of clinking glasses filled the room as the patrons stirred.

"I think Jeffrey has a musical future," I said.

"I agree. I'm glad you're enjoying the concert." Philip stuck a chip in the spinach dip and popped it in his mouth. "Hmm. That's good. Have some."

I reached for a serving as he sipped his tea. Moments such as these came and went with the blink of an eye, but I believed this one would etch a memory on my heart forever.

"You know, Lloyd's car reminds me of an old beater I owned as a teen," he said.

"What kind of car was it?"

"A light blue sports sedan, the snazziest vehicle I'd ever seen. My dad bought it for me from a neighbor."

Philip seemed to have led a cushy life on a level I knew little about. "What do you do in New York in your spare time?" I scooped up more spinach dip.

"Nothing as tranquil as this. I have to go to Narragansett Bay in Rhode Island to kick back. How about you?"

Since Jordan died other than an occasional dinner out with friends, I'd worked, read, or watched something boring on television. Philip's question forced me to think of the way things had been for Jordan and me. We took walks, went to plays in nearby Misty Gorge, and went out to nice restaurants. What was I thinking, telling myself I needed a change of scenery? I needed Jordan. This date was a bad idea. I wanted to go home. Tears rushed to my eyes. I blinked them back. "I uh..."

"I bet you read magazines about hairstyles."

Philip's caring tone soothed my frayed nerves. I laid my napkin beside my plate. "Yes, that's fun for me." If only he hadn't made me think of Jordan. My customers had told me I should go out, and I knew they meant the best for me, but there was no one for me but Jordan. I glanced at Philip. Maybe my clients were right. He wasn't proposing. It was only a distraction for one evening and the company was great. I took a deep breath and relaxed in my seat.

Jeffrey returned and played several Bach church cantatas. Then he stood and pulled a small notepad out of his tuxedo jacket pocket. "While you enjoy a delicious dessert, please call out the titles of songs you like. We'll end with a sing-along."

His fingers flew across the pad as guests fired names while a waiter carrying a silver tray deposited a chocolate mousse by each place setting.

"These are great selections. Thanks for your enthusiasm." Jeffrey flipped up the tails on his jacket, sat down, and pulled up the piano bench. Happy melodies filled the room as his fingers lightly tapped the keys making the tunes dance with his signature style. The audience's voices grew louder and more enthusiastic with each song until finally he stopped, stood, and took a bow.

Philip and I rose from our seats and joined the wide-eyed men and women giving him a standing ovation. No wonder. By the time his performance ended, it had sent me soaring high above my hum-drum everyday life, and I was glad I'd agreed to go on this date.

When the clapping finally ceased, Philip guided me out amid a mix of fruity perfume and woodsy aftershave wafting from grand ladies and gentlemen. We slid into the old vehicle. He glanced at the key then me before he started the engine. But he drove down the mountain into a sleepy town with no hitches. Only the lampposts lining the streets lit the way for the old car, humming along on the level roads. I pinched myself to make sure this night wasn't a dream as the pebbles in my drive crunched under the vehicle's tires.

Philip parked, let me out of the passenger's seat, and put his arm around my waist.

Warmth tingled over my skin as he escorted me to the door. His gaze searched my face as he pulled me close. He brushed his lips against mine, and Jordan popped in my head. I turned away, but Philip reached for me and kissed my cheeks. Then his lips found their way to mine. Ecstasy I hadn't known since Jordan died and never thought I'd know again pulsed through my veins. He let go and brushed back my hair. "What about tomorrow?"

How much heartache would a sudden separation from the bliss I'd just experienced cause? The deeper Philip burrowed into my soul the more it would hurt when he left, but I yearned for the joy he brought. "Would you like to go to church?"

Philip let go and stared at me with wide, surprised eyes, but in a moment he said, "Yes."

I put my hand on the doorknob. "It starts at eleven o'clock. If you pick me up, we'd better allow extra time for that thing to get up the hill."

Philip chuckled. "I'll see you at ten-thirty."

Jordan always told me I was a dreamer and shouldn't get suckered by things too good to be true. How much could a person get suckered in a worship service?

5

Philip whistled a happy tune as he entered his room. The swirling-designed burgundy curtains with motel-thick backing blocked the lights from the parking lot. He switched on the lamp then slung his suit jacket over the office chair in front of the desk.

Images of Eve filled his brain. She'd been so gracious about everything, bringing him coffee in the midst of all that wreckage. The kindness he'd seen in her eyes told him beauty lived inside her. And at the concert. Oh yeah, she was the hottest woman there. Spending time with her was as good as a day on Narragansett Bay. He lived for those times of peace when he escaped the hustle of the job. Who would've thought he'd ram his car into Eve's Clips and find tranquility in such an unlikely place?

The dark screen on his laptop reminded him to catch up with work. Thankful for the reception at the motel for his cell phone and computer, he plopped down. How many e-mails could he have on Saturday night? Touching the ON button he waited. Fifty. Didn't these people ever take a break? He clicked the first one.

Dear Philip,

My portfolio has been performing poorly. Please call me. I'd like to discuss other options with you and compare them to new possibilities I've gotten from another company.

Best,

Valerie Klingman

Philip's muscles tensed. But Valerie Klingman wouldn't spoil the remains of this perfect evening.

An "Inside Triville" pamphlet lying beside his computer caught his eye. He snatched it, ambled to the bed and propped on a pillow. Ah-ha, a picture of the diner. Yeah. The one where Eve and he went. He revisited the coziness of the place and the evening. Eve's personality sparkled like a diamond, the real thing. He'd been dating cubic zirconias. His eyes grew heavy, and the paper fell from his hands. He took off his shirt and pants, crawled under the comforter, and fell asleep.

~*~

Philip slapped at the buzzing alarm clock until it shut up. He sat on the side of the bed and rubbed his head as visions of coffee flashed in his mind. Ahh, a fancy coffee maker. He meandered over and popped in a hazelnut packet. The machine whirred as it worked its magic, and a sweet aroma filled the room.

A complimentary newspaper lay on the floor in front of the door. Sipping his drink, he wandered to the few thin pages and picked them up. Not much happening. No wonder he'd slept better here.

Not only that, it was beyond all reason, but he'd been more content amid the crisis in Eve's Clips than he was on most work days in New York. Until he'd visited here the thing he most wanted from life was rest at Narraganset Bay. Odd, but now that wouldn't be enough. These magnificent hills turned his nerves to calm the same way the peaceful body of water in

Rhode Island did, but he'd found a sense of security here he hadn't known since Dad died, and he didn't know why.

After a while would Triville bore him? The residents moved at such a slow pace or perched on their porches and watched the clouds float by. Yet, his soul longed for something they possessed. If only he understood what. Even if he didn't, he'd never tire of seeing Eve. He dropped down into the chair.

A large color photo of a woman weaving a basket announced the Western Hills Festival. He'd never been to a mountain gala, and Monday was Eve's day off, not that she could work in the wreckage he'd left in her shop. Guilt pricked his skin. Then he remembered church.

He slung the paper to the floor, tugged on a pair of gray pants and a blue dress shirt, and walked outdoors into bright sunshine streaming through the pine trees. No telling how long it would take to crank the old vehicle. The manager meandered by and patted Philip on the shoulder. "Hope you slept well last night."

People here certainly were friendly. "Yes, fine. Thank you." Philip got in the car, turned the key, and held his breath.

The engine started right up and he exhaled. She hummed on the level road and he arrived at Eve's without a hitch. He whistled a happy tune as he trekked to the door. She answered, and he couldn't keep his gaze from wandering from her dark sparkling eyes to her stunning black top and skirt complimenting her curvy body. "I-uh-uh like your outfit." *Geez, I'm tongue-tied*. He'd never live that down if his friends in New York could hear him. Had the thin air affected him?

"You look rather handsome yourself."

He couldn't have stopped his lips from spreading into a wide grin if he'd wanted to. He held out his arm and escorted Eve to the passenger's side. He scooted into his seat and rubbed his hands together. *Aggravating car*. He stiffened his jaw. "OK, where to?"

"It's on top of a hill." Eve mumbled the words.

Philip laughed to conceal his nervousness as he started the car. It would make a fool of him yet. He wouldn't care if it didn't do it in front of Eve. "It's all right. We'll manage."

He backed out, and they rode along past the renovated stores and shops lining Main Street.

"There. Turn right at the post office." Eve pointed to a red brick building.

Philip clenched his teeth and headed up a steep hill lined with sycamore trees and wild pink azaleas. The car slowed then jerked. Eve's gorgeous looks and the car embarrassing him tied his brain in knots. Did she think he wasn't man enough to handle the old car? Lloyd had probably loaned the vehicle to every guy in Triville, and more than likely they all knew how to maneuver it up steep grades.

"Floor it." Eve gave him a pointed look as though she understood.

He might as well have been on Mars driving a space ship. "Good idea." He mashed the pedal. The car almost cut out, but rumbled to the pebble lot in front of a white, wood-frame church. His chest filled with pride for the accomplishment as he cut the engine. He zipped around upstate New York effortlessly in his luxury sedan. Why was this more fun?

He patted the steering wheel, slid out, and opened Eve's door. She flashed a big smile as though she appreciated his effort to get them here, his manners, or both.

They followed a walkway of large flat stones to the entrance, where he grabbed hold of a black, wrought iron handle on a plank door and pulled it open.

Eve's high heels clicked on the hardwood floor as she sauntered to a pew with a burgundy cushion. Bonnie Sue sat two rows in front of them amid four people Philip had never seen. She turned around, grinned, and mouthed, "Hi, handsome."

Hoping Eve hadn't noticed Bonnie Sue's greeting, Philip gave Bonnie Sue a half-nod and plunked down by Eve.

Someone tapped Philip on the shoulder.

Lloyd was all dressed up in a navy pin-striped suit. "Good to see ya', Philip."

"Thanks."

Lloyd directed his gaze toward Eve. "How's it going in the shop?"

"They're making progress." Eve sounded less than hopeful.

Philip wished he could undo the wreck. He'd still want to meet Eve, but there had to be a better way.

Lloyd sat in front of them.

The regal sounds of the opening hymn rang out from a ten-person choir. They marched down the middle aisle and took their seats behind the minister by the time the song ended.

The lanky preacher rose from his chair at the front of the pulpit and stepped to the lectern. "Good morning."

The congregation answered, "Good morning."

The minister opened the Bible. "In Matthew twenty-two, verses thirty-seven through forty a

Pharisee asked Jesus to tell him the greatest commandment in the law. "Jesus replied:—'Love the Lord your God with all your heart and with all your soul and with all your mind.' This is the first and greatest commandment. And the second is like it: 'Love your neighbor as yourself...'" The pastor closed the Good Book. "'Love your neighbor as yourself.' Were you a blessing to anyone this past week? You don't have to answer out loud or even raise your hand."

Philip looked at Eve's small, smooth hand lying in her lap. He reached over and squeezed it. She was different from the women he'd dated in New York, the opposite of the Valerie Klingmans in his life who wouldn't go out of their way to aid a stranger. Once Valerie learned he had only a small amount of time to spend with her, she begrudged his work, called him a player, and broke up with him. That was hurtful and insulting.

It wasn't an issue with Eve. She wasn't trying to tie him down or take advantage of his position in life. He smiled to himself. Did people here understand position?

"God wants us to offer our fellow man and woman friendship. Perhaps our neighbor's not the most likeable person in town. But what is his burden? Even if we don't know, we treat him or her as God says."

The residents of Triville lived by this man's words. Acceptance of others in this busy world was rare. Many, like his boss, tolerated people for business reasons. He knew for a fact George didn't care for the company's web designer, but that IT guy was so talented. George took him, the secretaries, and the stockbrokers out to eat occasionally, and they all made small talk over steak at one of the fancy restaurants. Libby March, the receptionist, irritated Richard Ford, another stockbroker at the company, because she couldn't keep his clients straight when she buzzed in his calls, but at the last dinner he sat beside her and talked to her as though she was his best friend.

Genuine, sincere people attended this church. They cared. He might never have seen the difference if he hadn't crashed his car into Eve's Clips.

Bulletins rustled and brought Philip's thoughts to the moment. He and Eve stood with the congregation and the minister gave them a blessing. The choir sang a parting hymn. Then the parishioners filed into the aisles. He and Eve followed them to the rock stoop and Reverend Binder.

Reverend Binder shook Philip's hand as Eve said, "This is Philip Wells. He's here to..."

"Welcome, Mr. Wells. Mr. Jacobsen's sister was in the diner on Friday, when I was having my morning coffee. I overheard her mention to Bonnie Sue that you were here from New York to see Corley. Bonnie Sue told her you had crashed into Eve's shop."

Philip's lips parted, but he snapped them shut.

Reverend Binder's eyes twinkled as though he was amused he'd shocked Philip. "It takes a while to learn our ways, but we grow on people."

Had Philip grown on Eve? "I'm catching on, and the diner's a great place to do it." He turned his gaze toward Eve. "Let's go there for lunch."

Eve's lips curled into a smile.

"An excellent idea. Make up for the accident." Approval rang in Reverend Binder's tone.

Philip went toward the parking lot, the pebbles

crunching underneath his shoes.

Eve looked over her shoulder. "Philip wants to see Bonnie Sue." She spoke toward the preacher as though her words were meant for him. Yet they were too far away for the minister to hear.

Maybe Eve *had* noticed his and Bonnie Sue's exchange when they entered the church. He gritted his teeth. No one would come between him and Eve. "I do *not* want to see Bonnie Sue."

Eve chuckled as Philip opened the passenger door and helped her in.

He took the wheel at the driver's seat, started the engine, and backed out. Was Eve making fun of Bonnie Sue? That was hardly called for, and out of character for Eve. "Are you laughing at Bonnie Sue?"

"I suppose in a way everybody does, but she amuses others because she flirts with everyone. I imagine anyone she hasn't hit on either feels left out or undesirable."

Ahh. Apparently Bonnie Sue had created her own reputation. At the same time, those who knew her appeared to accept her. The people of Triville had gotten the same hold on Philip as they had on each other. He didn't understand how, but it mattered not. He was only passing through town. "I wouldn't want to be in either category." He patted the wheel. "We're coasting down the mountainside."

The car sailed to the bottom of the hill and through town, but chugged, and sputtered on the way to the diner. The vehicle complained, but kept going. Would it hold up as long as he needed it to? More importantly, how did the people of Triville's ways pertain to Eve? Would she ignore Bonnie Sue and continue to go out with him?

6

The smell of French fries tickled my nostrils as I entered Bob's Diner with Philip.

Delores Witt, a junior in high school with aspirations of becoming a nurse waved from behind the cash register. "Come on in. How ya'll doin'?" Delores's sweet voice barely carried over the people chattering at the counter.

"Hi. Fine, thank you." I returned her gesture, and we scooted into the second booth.

Bonnie Sue hurried over tying the sash on her apron. She stood next to Philip and batted those long eyelashes. "I just made it here from church. You're my first customer, handsome."

"As long as there's a chili cheeseburger waiting for me." Philip's words pointed to his interest in lunch, not Bonnie Sue.

She directed her gaze toward me, but without the flirty eyes. Philip hadn't fallen into her trap, and he didn't even know the words "biggest flirt" appeared under her name in the high school yearbook. What a smart man. "Sounds good. I'll have one too."

I tried to smile at her, but I think I smirked. What was wrong with me? Getting jealous over a man I hardly knew. From high school until the day Jordan died, I loved only him. I wanted him to hold me when I was sad and laugh with me when I was happy. He'd never do that again. A sinking sensation hit me in the gut.

I glanced at Philip. He leaned across the table and stared at me. I couldn't deny he stirred something inside me. Did happiness knock on the door of my heart for the first time in years? Did I dare let it in knowing it was only for a short time? Either way, I had to stop resenting Bonnie Sue. Who could blame her?

Philip rested his chin on his fist. "What are you up to this afternoon?"

"I'll probably take a nap then prepare something simple for dinner." Maybe he'd want to come over. "Would you like to join me?"

His blue eyes lit up. "Sure, what time?"

"About six o'clock." My parents had instilled hospitality in me, but I'm sure they had counted on me to temper it with common sense. If my heart broke when Philip left Triville, I had no one to blame but myself.

Lloyd ambled over and shook Philip's hand. "That car still working for ya'?"

"It's humming like a songbird." Philip kept a straight face.

Lloyd slapped his knee, tilted his head back, and laughed. "Eve, he's all right."

Was Lloyd giving his approval for me to see Philip? Was it that obvious that he'd awakened a yearning inside me? My heart skipped a beat for all the pain it would cause when Philip left. I had to stop seeing him before the ache would be too much to bear, and to think, I'd just invited him to my home.

Lloyd ran his hand through his hair. "The part for the car I'm repairin' should get here next week. As soon as I have it, we'll get 'er fixed."

"It could be a month before I leave." Philip's grin

spread across his face.

He must've liked the idea of staying here a while, but in thirty days he'd be gone, and I'd never see him again. What was I thinking? Heaviness formed in my chest. Then a bell rang in my head. There'd be no commitment for either of us. That meant no betrayal of Jordan and no guilt. I deserved a few nights of fun, didn't I?

"We'll have it for ya' for sure by then."

"Thank you, sir."

"You bet." Lloyd took a step to my side of the booth and tapped my shoulder. "Hang in there, Eve. Pete and Charlie will make your place as good as new." He headed to the back and Bonnie Sue set our steaming plates on the table.

Philip bit into his lunch, his mouth half grinning as he chewed. "Hmm. I don't think I've ever eaten a burger this good."

"I guess I take them for granted, ordering one anytime I want."

"Triville should be known for the country's best chili cheeseburger," Philip said.

"I don't know about that. If we wanted to give it the title we'd have to go to every community in the United States and eat chili cheeseburgers."

Philip sat back in his chair and laughed. "We should do that."

What a frivolous thing to say. We didn't have enough time to travel to even a few nearby places before he returned to New York. Triville wasn't real to him. I wasn't real to him. I slumped in my seat, blinking my eyelids, squeezing back the tears rushing to my eyes.

He ate his last French fry. "I hate to leave when

I'm having so much fun, but I have work to do." He left Bonnie Sue a five-dollar tip, stood, and picked up the bill.

I rose from my seat, and we went to the cash register. My head knew he'd leave for good one day. How could I let my heart ignore it?

In what seemed only moments we went outside and got in the car. We sailed down the hill and level roads leading to my house, and Philip escorted me to the door. He pushed back a tendril of hair on my forehead. Lightly etching the side of my face with his hand, he placed his soft lips on mine. His breathing increased and joy fell over me while my heart beat next to his. He pulled away and stroked my cheek.

"See you later, gorgeous." He turned and headed toward the car, leaving my mind longing for one more moment of happiness before I stopped this relationship that never could be.

I hurried to the kitchen and pulled Aunt Rose's instructions for beef tips over rice from a book with a tattered red cloth cover and papers sticking out of it at odd angles. Perfect, but I had to allow time for the beef to marinate. I laid down the handwritten notes and tore out to the car.

After a quick trip to the grocery I returned and stood at my counter top with a sirloin tip roast and my chef's knife. I chopped the meat into bite-sized pieces, and set it aside. Aunt Rose's secret sauce made the entree melt in one's mouth. I added it and placed the dish in the fridge.

Music rang out from the radio as I polished my silver tray and arranged cheese and crackers on it. The clock ticked to four, and I danced around the room while I waited for Aunt Rose's concoction to finish its magic. I hadn't done that in ages, but the steps, the joy came back to me. The song ended, and I pulled out the seasoned delicacy.

I dipped juicy looking cubes of meat from the dripping liquid and browned them and the onions. To wrap up the meal, I poured in the remaining marinade, turned the burner to low, and prepared rice. Now for an elegant setting.

I retrieved a blue-checked tablecloth and napkins from the linen chest. They blended with the border on the plates my grandmother gave me. Only the centerpiece was missing. I marched into the kitchen and snatched the arrangement of dogwood blossoms in the blue vase from the windowsill in front of the sink. Then I plunked it down on the dining room table and placed blue candles on either side of it. Looked like New York to me.

~*~

The doorbell rang.

"Hi, I'm so glad you could come." I pointed toward the den. "Have a seat."

Phillip sank down on the sofa, and I left the room. My heart danced as I brought in a tray of hors d'oeuvres. "I'll be right with you." I returned to the kitchen and came back with two big glasses of sweet tea.

Philip sipped his drink. "Umm. Good."

"I'm glad you like it." I joined him, picked up a cheese cracker, and munched it. "Did you have any trouble getting here?"

"No, I didn't have to climb a hill." He snickered.

"Maybe it won't be long until Lloyd has your rent-a-car repaired."

"*Pff.* That car's fun to drive. Now I admit, at first I worried it might quit on me, but it doesn't appear to be a problem." Philip set his glass on the coaster.

I wanted to ask if he'd visit Triville after he snagged Mr. Jacobsen's account, but the words stuck in my throat. "I'm sure running around these hills in that vehicle has been quite an experience."

Philip chuckled. "One I won't easily forget."

Would he remember the times we'd shared here? "You'll have lots of memories—crashing into a beauty shop, driving a clunker that keeps humming in spite of itself, and of course, there's Mr. Jacobsen." A twinge of pain pricked my heart when I said Mr. Jacobsen's name. Once Philip met him and secured his business, there'd be no more memories for him and me.

"All good. At least, I hope Mr. Jacobsen and I will get along and our meeting will go well."

"I'm sure it will."

"So, you don't cook much on Sundays."

Aunt Rose's beef tips hardly could pass for a simple dish. At the same time, I didn't want Philip to know how much I yearned to impress him. "After you left, a recipe that's been in my family for years popped in my head, and I couldn't resist."

"It smells delicious." Philip tapped the rim of his tea glass. "I'll have this with dinner if you don't mind."

"Sure. I already placed fresh ones on the dining room table. Sounds as if you're ready to eat."

"With the aroma wafting in here it's hard not to be."

"Let's go." I smiled and floated on his compliment as I guided him to the home-cooked meal. The quiet room and centerpiece lent an intimacy Bob's Diner lacked. I scooted in the seat across from Philip and fanned my face from the warmth pulsing from my heart. Did Philip experience it too?

"Should I say grace?" he asked.

"Yes, please."

Philip said a blessing then picked up his fork and scooped up a bite of rice.

I'd stuffed in so many meals by myself at the kitchen table. Looking at him seemed like an illusion.

Philip speared a forkful of beef tips. "Hmm. This is so good."

"Thank you."

"Do you enjoy cooking gourmet dishes?"

It'd been fun preparing this one because he was coming to dinner. "I like it fine when I have time, and I'm in the mood."

"You must have been in the mood today. This is great."

Heat rushed to my face, not at the praise, but at the affection in his voice. Was I reading more into it than he meant? His searching gaze told me I wasn't. Who'd have thought someone like Philip would turn up in this little mountain town and have a meal in my house?

"Is this a secret recipe?" Philip wiggled his eyebrows when he said the word secret.

"It's my great Aunt Rose's special marinade."

Philip placed his napkin on the table. "It was incredible."

I carried our plates to the kitchen and brought in homemade brownies and coffee. I'd never entertained a date in this house. Jordan loved my cooking, but we were married when we built our home. Now there was an attractive man from New York in my dining room, and he wasn't just any man. He drew me into him as though he'd cast a spell over me. I hardly could believe this evening was real.

Philip popped a sweet treat in his mouth. "Umm." He picked up his coffee cup and sipped.

"When will you go back to New York?" I made polite conversation, but my words sent an ache to my chest.

"As soon as I finalize things with Mr. Jacobsen."

Finalize! I couldn't do this. I had to stop seeing him.

He pushed aside his dessert plate. "That was delicious—beyond words."

"Thank you." I picked up our dishes and carried them to the kitchen as he wandered into the den. I set them down then joined him.

A hairstylist magazine I hadn't noticed earlier when I'd brought in the hors d'oeuvres lay next to him on the sofa. A fine, distinguished man like Philip sitting next to a periodical with pictures of hairdos. My face grew hot. I'd been so busy setting the stage for my New York act I'd left a piece of the real me lying around.

He picked it up and flipped a few pages. "Some of these styles are pretty wild."

I snatched it from him and sat down. "I'm sorry I don't have a news magazine."

"That's OK. I'd rather look at you." He pulled me close.

Snuggling into his chest I found a safe, comfortable place and yearned to stay there. He ran his finger down my cheek, his tender touch melting my heart. His lips brushed against mine, and I put my arms around his neck. My emotions twirled.

He released me and touched the tip of my nose with his forefinger. "How did you get so cute?"

My stern will to resist his charms turned to mush. "You're not bad yourself."

"Then you might say 'yes' if I asked you to go to the Western Hills Festival with me tomorrow. I saw an article about it in the paper. It looks interesting."

"Sure. That'll be fun." Had I really said those words? It would be rude to back out, and I didn't want to, but each time I saw Philip I gave him another little piece of my heart.

"I should go and turn in. I'll pick you up around eleven o'clock."

He stood, and I escorted him to the entrance. He gave me a peck on the lips then opened the door and disappeared into the night.

I locked up and leaned against the wall like a moonstruck teenager. One day he'd go out for good. My plan not to see him seemed so simple until I was with him. By agreeing to go with him tomorrow and kissing him goodnight I'd dug a deeper hole for my emotions to fall into. Tomorrow I'd stand firm and end this once and for all.

7

The sun shone on two bread slices with turkey, provolone, lettuce, and tomatoes generously stuffed between them. Two sodas sat beside them on the white kitchen counter. Tin foil rattled and a sweet aroma wafted up as I wrapped leftover brownies.

I picked up the sandwiches and sweet treats, placed them in a picnic basket, and snapped the lid. The doorbell rang, and I hung the carrier on my wrist, stuffed the drinks into a small cooler, and trekked to the door.

"Hi, thanks for bringing our lunch. After last night I know whatever's in there is good." Philip's lips turned up on the corners as he reached out and took items from me.

"You're welcome. The restaurants in New York must have lots of delicious dishes." I headed toward the old car with New York on my mind. I'd told myself before this day ended I'd gather my nerve and let Philip know I couldn't see him again. When I was with him so much joy surrounded me I forgot life's harsh realities, especially the one in which he'd leave and break my heart. I had to stand firm.

"Not as good as the ones I've eaten here."

Philip placed our lunch in the car's backseat. I peered at the sheet of plastic covering my shop window and the part of the wall missing the bricks. I breathed deep trying to overcome the helplessness sinking into my pores. I'd left a key under a big rock beside the door in case Pete and Charlie showed up. They had to.

Philip let me into the car and I stiffened as he took the driver's seat. Would the old vehicle take us to the festival? She grunted and groaned winding up the mountain road but lived up to the task.

I motioned toward the first picnic station under the shade of oak and sycamore trees by the river. "Stop there. It's probably past your lunchtime."

"No argument. I plead hungry." Philip pulled onto the parking area beside a patch of emerald green grass and two mountain laurel bushes and cut the engine. We eased out of the car, and I set the wicker basket on the seat attached to the table.

English sparrows flew from it and scattered as I unlatched the top of the container. The loose hinges on the lid wiggled when I opened it. I pulled out the red and white checked tablecloth, and a mountain breeze carrying the scent of moist, fresh earth blew by and furled it. I whipped it in place, added the napkins, and plopped the basket on it as an anchor.

Philip swatted at a fly.

Nothing would interrupt this perfect picnic. I'd keep it in my memory forever. I pulled out a citronella candle and lit it. "Would you like to say a blessing?"

"Sure."

We bowed our heads.

"Our Heavenly Father, thank you for this beautiful day and for time to relax. Thank you for Eve who prepared this food. Bless it to the nourishment of our bodies. In Christ's name we pray. Amen."

Philip rubbed his hands together and wiggled his eyebrows. "Now to eat." He took a bite of his sandwich. "I've never dined next to a river flowing at ground level."

Crystal clear water babbled over rocks in the riverbed lined with white trillium and wild pink azaleas. Salamanders and trout swam downstream and a frog croaking mixed with tweets from the birds in the distance. I soaked in nature's bounty and stress rolled off me like raindrops.

"Some people drink from it. They claim the stream rushes too fast for lizards, snakes, and such to contaminate it, and there aren't any pollutants up here."

"I'd like a few sips from the spring. Is that it spurting from those two boulders?" Philip pointed upstream to the other side of the river.

I glanced over my shoulder. "Yes. That's where the water comes from."

We finished eating, cleaned the table, and hiked up the narrow trail that wound through underbrush and wild flora. Sticks crunched underneath our shoes and leaves rustled until we stood on the riverbank facing the spring on the opposite side.

Philip tilted his head and stared at the water. "Do we wade over?"

"We can walk. See." I motioned toward the stones stretching across the water.

"Wouldn't we be better off wading? We might fall."

Obviously, Philip hadn't grown up near the great outdoors. I put my hand on my hip. "Well, yeah, if you plan on slipping."

Philip bit his bottom lip as though he thought better of his suggestion to drink from the spring. Even if he did, he'd cart himself across that river. He didn't seem the type of man to back down. "OK, you're right. We'll go one at a time. Usually it's ladies first, but I'll let you choose."

I'd crossed here many times. If I led the way, he could follow my path. The last thing I wanted him to do was misstep and take a tumble. "I'll go."

I grabbed a low-hanging branch on an oak tree and leapt to the first rock. Balancing with my arms I trod the short distance to the second. One wide stride took me to the slab on the other side in front of the spring. I peered over my shoulder.

Philip stood on stone number two. Secure on the large boulder, I turned around and waved him over. "Come on."

He bounded over and landed right beside me. He flashed a grin so big it looked as though it might crack his cheeks. We stood for a moment then bent down and scooped up handfuls of natural spring water.

"It's so beautiful here." Philip swung his arm toward the river. Then, he pulled me close and I melted into his arms. He brushed his lips against mine then deepened his kiss. I swirled with the roar of the waterfall. Cool, moist droplets splashed onto us from the cascade, and I rose like the swell of the river and floated to a place I'd never been.

He released me and took my hand. "This is the best part of the Western Hills Festival." He looked at the surroundings then me. "I would offer to carry you across but…"

He'd already transported me where I never intended to go. "Go ahead. I'm right behind you."

Stepping carefully, we reached dry ground. Philip leaned over, picked up several pebbles, and skipped them across the rippling water. The joy he brought and the pain his leaving would cause sent my emotions crashing faster than the current. Had he experienced the swell of the river? Did he want it to never end?

He brushed off his palms and clasped my hand as we strolled to the old car. A short drive took us to a stoneware display. We got out and proceeded to a woman with short, curly black hair seated at a pottery wheel. A mound of clay spun around and around on the throwing device while she touched the vessel with both hands shaping it. The sun glinted off one of the finished pieces, and it caught my eye. An iris that looked as though it grew on the side of a vegetable bowl with a royal blue band testified to the artist's talent.

Philip smiled at her. "I've never watched pottery in progress before. Thank you for demonstrating."

"You're welcome."

We left and drove to a parking space farther into town. A wooden replica of a pioneer woodsman dressed in buckskin holding a rifle stood guard over a two-story inn. I studied the long tail on his fur cap as we got out of the old vehicle. It appeared a coyote had donated its skin.

We continued down the street past a faux black bear and entered a store with a log cabin front. The scent of moss mixed with pine filled the air. Handmade baskets covered the ceiling. More stoneware dishes, small beaded purses, and handmade rugs sat on the shelves. I studied a pair of brown, tear-drop earrings peppered with tiny copper-colored specks lying on a display counter. Then I picked them up and wandered past shelves of colorful quilts to reach the clerk, an attractive woman with high cheek bones. The light bounced off the earrings. "These are so pretty. What are they made of?"

Philip leaned close to me and gazed at them. "I believe those are quartz."

"Yes, the semi-precious gemstones come from this area. We cut and polish them."

Philip pulled his wallet out of his pants pocket. "We'll take them."

"Philip, that's not nec..." I had to stop him. How could I accept a gift from him when I intended to tell him not to call me? The strength to say the words escaped me every time I was with him, or I wouldn't have been here today.

The lady promptly took hold of the jewelry, rang up the sale, and handed me the purchase. "I hope you enjoy these."

"I'm sure I will." I turned toward Philip. "What a nice surprise. Thank you." It was all I could do to keep tears from spilling over my eyelashes. This kind man burrowed further into my heart every time I went out with him. Soon it would be too late to turn back, impossible to not see him. I had to take care of it today.

"A little something for showing me around." He flashed a satisfied-looking grin as though giving me a gift made him happy.

What a sweet guy. God put one of us in the wrong place. We walked outside, and the bright sunshine nearly blinded me, but I put on my sunglasses to shield my misty eyes. If only I didn't know the pain of losing someone I loved, maybe I could embrace each moment with Philip. Most women had dated at least three times more men than I had and never experienced the heartache I carried every day. I couldn't add to it.

The sound of a fast-paced tune filled the air. We turned a corner and joined a crowd gathered around a group of women wearing tap shoes on a stage. The ladies donned short light blue dresses with poufy skirts. They weren't performing a traditional rendition as Fred Astaire would. Instead they formed in a line and clicked the toes and heels of their shoes in staccato movements. In unison they swung their left legs over their right in what resembled an Irish jig.

Philip stared at them with intense eyes. Then he turned to me. "What are they doing?"

"In this area folks call it clogging. I understand some refer to it as buck dancing. The dance form originated in these mountains when the Irish, Scottish, English, and Dutch-German settlers arrived. They toe-tapped to the fiddle or bluegrass music and the dances from their countries merged to create clogging. The word clog means time. The dancers keep rhythm with the downbeat with their heels."

I watched their feet and the fast pace mesmerized me until Philp said, "Wow. That was great."

He grasped my hand, and we meandered to the other end of the block. A fiddler dressed in jeans and a red plaid shirt played a snappy tune while eight men and women square-danced. The men wore blue jeans and western style red shirts with gold ribbing. The dancing ladies had on gold blouses and red skirts that swished just below their knees when they turned.

Those participating joined hands and walked forward with their elbows bent. Then the caller instructed, "Circle left."

They formed a circle keeping time to the music in that direction until the caller sent them to the right. Then he declared, "Right and Left Grand." They continued in the circle, but passing each other and clasping hands until he instructed them to Do Si Do.

Each of the four couples faced their partners, passed right shoulders, slid back to back and ended up in front of one another.

"Looks like fun." Philip tugged at my elbow then guided me beyond the woman demonstrating how to weave a basket as the happy music faded behind us.

I was glad he'd brought me with him. If we had nothing else, we'd have memories from the time we spent here. I'd been to many Western Hill Festivals, but today I was with Philip. His open innocence like that of a child, a side of him I hadn't seen, endeared him to me even more.

Philip and I crossed the street and headed up the other side of the village amid the vendors' smells of popcorn and cotton candy. Philip kicked at a pebble on the sidewalk. "I lack the freedom to think. Uh, I didn't mean that the way it sounded. I think all the time about stocks, numbers, and portfolios, but I don't contemplate the world around me."

"That's true of lots of us. A hymn about this being God's world comes to mind every time I visit here, and I can't help but repeat the words from Psalm 19, the one that says, 'The heavens declare the glory of God; the skies proclaim the work of his hands.' I think it's because I stop bustling around, breathe in the wonder of the lush green hills meeting the blue sky, and relish the cool breeze on my cheeks.

Wrinkles creased Philip's brow. "After spending time here, I almost feel like a computer, as though I've been programmed to live a certain way."

Here was my opportunity. "I don't know if that's true or not, but we do have different lives. I've been thinking about that."

Philip's eyebrows shot up as he helped me in the

passenger's side of the car. He scooted into the driver's seat and tilted his head. "You've been thinking about our lives?" Shock lined his voice.

Maybe in his mind we hardly knew each other, but this relationship, or whatever we had, had crashed into my life the same way his vehicle hit my shop. I couldn't live with the emotional wreckage it could bring any more than I could the bashed-in wall and window. "Yes, I wonder if we should keep seeing one another. You'll meet with Mr. Jacobsen soon then you'll be off to New York."

The corners of Philip's lips sagged as he turned on the engine and backed out. "I'd be so bored and lonely here without you."

Would he be bored and lonely in New York without me? "Naw, you've met lots of people. You know your way around. You'll find plenty to do."

Philip stared straight ahead. "I'm not looking for something to do. I want to see you."

A warm tingle skipped across my skin. Thinking logically was difficult around Philip, but he was like a dream. I'd wake up one day, and it'd be over. I had to plant my heart in reality. "We don't have much in common."

Philip drove down the mountain without speaking then pulled into my driveway and parked.

"Look, Pete and Charlie came today and put in the window." I flung the car door open and practically ran into my shop.

Philip followed and stood beside me.

"This is such a relief. They won't be in here tomorrow when I have customers."

"Sweetheart, they'll have to put up drywall and paint it."

The fire of excitement burning inside me for my shop the way it used to be dwindled like a flickering flame as we strolled outside and I locked the door. "That's true, but I could ask them to come at night after I close."

"That would work." Philip put his hand behind my back and guided me to the house. "Please don't say you won't see me again." His eyes pleaded with me.

He'd leave and forget me. I had to be strong. "I'm sorry, Philip, but that's exactly what I'm saying."

He stuck out his hand. "It was nice meeting you, Eve Castleberry."

That's what I thought. I'd mean nothing to him once he left Triville. I shook his hand. "Likewise, Philip Wells."

His eyes looked damp.

Silent sobs erupted inside me as he plodded with slumped shoulders to the old car. I shut the door on the only man other than Jordan who'd ever touched my heart. I'd soon know how big an imprint he'd left on my life.

8

Maneuvering the old car on level ground, Philip sailed back to the motel as the sky turned twilight gray. He gazed at the hills towering around him and sensed his smallness. Loneliness swallowed him as he parked in front of his room. By rote he scooted out and lumbered underneath the yellow glow of the light by his door. The key clicked into a forlorn, silent night.

Inside he tossed the newspaper from the burgundy and gold comforter to the floor and fell face down on the bed. Beautiful Eve with her sparkling eyes and lovable personality never wanted to see him again, and for the most ridiculous reason. He lived in New York, and she resided in the South. What difference did that make? She claimed they had nothing in common. They enjoyed each other's company, had fun together. Wasn't that something in common?

Philip rubbed his head. Was the distance between New York and Triville a problem because she'd fallen in love with him and thought she needed to see him constantly? Was he in love with her? He'd had a good time dating Valerie Klingman, but it wasn't the same as it was with Eve. Eve's tenderness pulled at him like a magnet. Just seeing her set his heart on fire. As soon as he left her, he wanted to see her again.

Was that love? Had losing it yanked out his insides and make him queasy, or did he have food poisoning? He put his arms around his stomach to stop the ache from churning. Anything that caused this much pain couldn't be good for him. He'd honor Eve's wishes and not ask her out.

He swung his legs to the side of the bed, put his feet on the carpet then staggered to his computer and punched the ON button. The icons popped up as usual as if his world hadn't blown up. Another message from Valerie. Her complaints stirred up the bile in his gut even more. Often when life closed in on him, he sat back and sipped a cup of coffee. The magic potion gave him a new perspective. Or perhaps, it gave him time to adjust to things as they were.

He slogged to the machine and inserted a vanilla bean packet. The whirr jarred his aching head. The noise, which probably lasted only seconds, seemed to go on for an eternity. Finally, he reached for the cup, but the smell gagged him. He poured the libation in the sink. Servicing accounts was more important in this bad economy than ever before, but he couldn't do it right now. He leaned over and switched off the computer.

He changed into a pair of pajama bottoms, zigzagged to the bed, threw back the covers, and crawled under the sheet. He dozed off and on during the night, dreaming about Eve when she couldn't style Joyce's hair the way she wanted.

The look on her face. She was so cute, puckering her lips as she worked. Lips that called for him to kiss them as he had when they'd gone across the rocks to the natural spring. Agile, she'd danced over the boulders like a sprite as though she belonged to the landscape.

Tuesday morning he sat straight up in bed, perspiring, and choked up. Images of Valerie complaining about her portfolio and Eve telling him they couldn't see each other again whirled in his mind. His gaze drifted to the computer, but his heart flew to Eve. He grabbed the sides of his head. What was he? A wooly worm? No. He was a mountain lion.

He could fix the mileage problem. They weren't living in the olden days traveling by stage coach. He'd fly back and forth from New York to Merchantville. He couldn't desert Eve. After the disaster he created in her shop, what if she needed something?

He bounded out of bed, showered, and shaved. No suit needed in Triville. He dressed in a pair of jeans and a light blue shirt then pulled the office chair up to the table in front of the computer. The sooner he answered these e-mails the sooner he could see Eve.

Convincing Valerie he'd make a sound investment for her pressed on his mind. Placing his hands on the keyboard, he knew what he wanted to say, but he needed to phrase his correspondence to appease her.

Dear Valerie,

In these economic times I recommend stocks with little risk and good dividends. Go to our research page then let me know what you prefer. For security I suggest purchasing gold, silver, and possibly corporate stocks with a solid financial record. Consider my thoughts as well as yours then give me your selections. Together we'll make your portfolio work.

My Best Wishes for Your Continued Success,
Philip Wells

He rubbed his hands together and moved forward until he reached the end of the list he had labeled "Most Urgent." The other investors could wait until this afternoon. Eve's Clips should be open by now. He switched off his computer, dashed outside, and headed to the beauty shop. He intended to stay until Eve agreed to see him again.

~*~

I sat in the kitchen, the sun playing on the round pine table while my tears fell into hazelnut coffee. I shivered in the warmth of the morning as though it was thirty degrees in the kitchen. First Jordan gone—now this. How much heartache must I endure?

Did God send Philip to cheer me up and make me feel alive again? Or did Philip crash haphazardly into my life? Surely God would have sent someone for my future, not a person merely passing through Triville. God probably had nothing to do with it. What was I thinking taking up with a man who rammed a car into my beauty shop?

Why did it hurt so much? I hardly knew the guy. I grew up with Jordan. It wasn't a whirlwind, overnight romance. My dear Jordan. He'd waited for me until I finished my cosmetology course then we'd married, and he'd built the house and my beauty shop.

The shop. What time was it? Eleven already. I wiped my tears and headed outside. I still owned Eve's Clips. Butterflies danced in my stomach over having a customer in the disaster, but my eleven o'clock wanted to keep her appointment, and I was grateful. I couldn't neglect my clients and lose my livelihood.

I hiked across the porch onto the grass then crossed the pebble driveway. No sign of Pete and Charlie. I unlocked the door, and a musty smell hit my nostrils, probably from the sudsy water that had run all over the floor this past Friday. Philip had done such a good job cleaning it. I couldn't get him off my mind. Yet I couldn't deal with his unrealistic world, asking me out as though there was no tomorrow. Did he not care that he'd never see me again after Mr. Jacobsen returned?

Why did he have to come to Triville? No one ever came here except tourists. Tears rushed to my eyes. My goal for today—keep him out of my head. I wiped my cheeks and turned on the air conditioner. The stale odor disappeared.

Ellie Ringgold charged inside and set the curtain flying out from the window in the door. She swung her large yellow flowered purse as she approached me. "Hi, hon, I've been marking off the days to get this permanent. I want a loose wavy "'do."

"Absolutely." I stood beside the middle salon chair and patted it. "Let's get started."

She sat down, and I parted her locks in small portions and clipped them. I folded tissue paper over the first section, rolled it up, repeated the process and started to apply the permanent solution. "How's Smitty?"

"He's fine. Saturday night he's taking me to the Celebrate Triville Festival downtown. His brother's coming from Deerfield."

Some of the liquid trickled toward Ellie's ear. She stuck her smooth, slender hand out from under the burgundy cape and wiped it off. "Hon, I wish you'd go with us. Ask that good looking man who ran into your shop."

I jumped, yanked the roller, and quickly peered at her image in the mirror. She squinted as though she'd felt a twinge, but then her eyes softened into a sympathetic gaze. Apparently, she understood she'd upset me talking about Philip.

"It's all right for you to fall for someone. You're young. You've got a lot of life ahead of you."

Ahh. Ellie was one of the kindest people I knew. "You may be right, but not with this guy."

Ellie's auburn eyebrows shot up. "Why not? He seems friendly. I know he's not from here, but he appeared to adjust well to us." Ellie tilted her head. "I think he likes us."

How sweet. I couldn't help but chuckle. "Yeah, he does, but he'll leave soon." I dampened the last roller.

"If you charm him, he'll take you with him." Ellie stood and smoothed the burgundy cape.

I bounced her words around in my head. "I doubt he would. He's wrapped up in his work and tennis. There must be hundreds of ladies chasing after him in New York." My voice trailed off.

Ellie picked up a magazine from the fan-like display on the vanity. "Come on. Don't sell yourself short. You have lots to offer."

A smile bubbled inside me at Ellie's attempt to reassure me. "That's nice, but say you were right, and he asked me to go with him, I couldn't imagine myself living in New York. I'd be lost."

"If you're happy you can live anywhere. Nobody says you couldn't come home to visit." Wisdom lined Ellie's tone.

"I'll think about asking him to the festival."

Ellie padded to my desk and eased down in the chair with the flowered cushion. "You don't mind if I sit by your new window while this thing sets do you?"

"Of course not. Make yourself at home."

Inviting Philip anywhere was out of the question, but Ellie was only trying to be a good friend. That's one reason I'd said I'd think about it; the other, to keep her from throwing out ideas about Philip and me that stabbed my heart like knives.

I held the small white timer in my hand setting it for twenty minutes when the phone rang. Putting it down quickly, I answered. "Good morning. Eve's Clips."

"Hi, this is Pete. If you'll let us in after your last appointment, we'll hang the drywall tonight. That way, we'll be out of your hair. Hee-hee, no pun intended."

"Good one. It must be ESP. I'd hoped you might come this evening. I'll leave the key under the rock for you."

We hung up, and I sat in the hairstylist chair doodling with the box that had held Ellie's permanent solution. Where was the neutralizer? I ran my hand around inside the container. Empty.

I sprang out of my seat, tore to the back, and ripped the top off a box on my supply shelf. No neutralizer in there either. I opened all of the permanent kits and trembled in disbelief. In my mind's eye I saw Ellie's kinky hair. I stared at the useless supplies as though a bottle might appear if I gazed into them long enough. Instead images of tightly coiled, brown, blond, and auburn hair streaming from the containers popped in my head. I rubbed my face.

The neutralizer in a home perm would work. I dashed to the desk and grabbed the bag of money for making change from the top left drawer, being careful not to disturb Ellie. She glanced at me then stuck her nose back in the magazine.

I moved away from the desk and opened the sack. My heart fell—only four dollars. I slapped my forehead. I'd run out of checks. I didn't have time to drive to the drugstore, make the purchase, and wait for the cashier, Mandy Brown, to negotiate a credit transaction. She was so slow, not to mention how she jabbered during check-out. I shoved the money pouch back in the drawer.

Feeling faint, I dropped down in the chair at the shampoo bowl. I had to stop Ellie's hair from curling. The beauty shop was all I had. It was my life! My stomach tied in knots at the thought of losing my customers. I'd lost Jordan, and I could no longer look forward to seeing Philip. Of course, not seeing Philip was for the best, but I couldn't bear any more. I glanced at Ellie. She looked trusting and unassuming reading the periodical while the solution wreaked havoc on her hair. Tears lay heavy on my eyelashes.

The door slammed, and I flinched while Ellie looked up.

Philip stood there.

I nearly fell out of my chair.

Ellie's lips spread into a grin as big as her wave.

Philip returned Ellie's gesture, and she practically buried her face in the magazine as though she didn't want to infringe on mine and Philip's time together. What was he doing here?

My gaze locked with his as he wandered over to me. "You're as white as snow. What's wrong?"

In spite of everything I'd said about not wanting to go out with him, the sight of him and his caring tone comforted me like a cup of hot tea on a cold day. I got up and whispered in his ear. "I don-don-don't have neutralizer for Ellie's hair. I don't have time to go to the drugstore."

He gave me a hug. "How much does one cost?"

He spoke in a soft tone.

"Less than twenty dollars."

Philip pulled a small notepad from his shirt pocket and flipped it open. "Write what you need on here."

Fifteen minutes remained before I had to apply the neutralizer. It might work. I dabbed the tears from my eyes with my knuckle and did as he asked.

"No problem. I'll get that old car going in a hurry to the drugstore. Stop crying, gorgeous. It'll be all right." He dashed out, the door banging behind him. The engine sputtered and rumbled out of the driveway. How fast would it go?

The soft ticks of the clock rang in my ears like gongs. Three minutes gone. My hands perspired. There shouldn't be many people in the drugstore this time of day. I peered at the clock. Two more minutes had disappeared. What if Mandy wouldn't stop talking at the checkout counter? Four additional minutes. Barely able to breathe, I paced back and forth in front of the hairdresser's station.

Ellie stayed glued to her seat reading.

I glanced at the clock. Another four minutes passed. My heart thumped against my chest as I watched the second hand. Another minute lost— fourteen altogether. My heart sank.

Philip entered with a bag at his side.

I focused on Ellie. The magazine still covered her face.

"Here ya' go." Philip handed me the package.

I pulled out the neutralizer with a shaky hand, and he hurried toward the bathroom. In only seconds he'd deposit the container on the supply shelf out of sight. My hero. I tapped Ellie on the shoulder, and she flinched. "Time to neutralize your curls."

My heart slowed to a near normal pace as she laid down the magazine, stood, and sauntered to the hairstylist chair.

Philip emerged from the storage area and joined us.

Ellie rose up slightly and shook hands with him. "Ellie Ringgold. It's so nice to see you again. I don't think Eve introduced us the other night at Bob's Diner. I was sitting right in front of you." Ellie got a mischievous look in her eyes. "Do you come by often to visit the restroom at Eve's Clips?"

I wanted to cover my head with a towel, but at least her conversation gave me a few moments to settle my nerves.

Philip's neck turned red. "Yes, well, no, I actually came to ask Eve to go out with me tonight."

Ellie grabbed the neutralizer and dabbed it on her hair. "Don't let me interfere with that."

Philip probably thought I was desperate for a date, and that Triville had a shortage of men.

I snatched the solution from Ellie. "Actually, I think Philip dropped by to see if Mr. Jacobsen has called. Didn't you?" I flashed him a harsh look.

His lips turned down as he shut his eyes halfway. He'd been so kind. How could I make him sad? I couldn't, and I owed him big time for making the trip to the drugstore. "But if he wanted to ask me out I probably could go." How weak I'd become over a bottle of neutralizer.

Ellie glared at me. "Of course, you could. What else are you doing on a Tuesday night in Triville?"

I wanted to crawl under the shampoo bowl. "Pete and Charlie are coming after my last appointment to put up drywall."

"How about that rock outside your door only a few people in town know about? They could look under it." Ellie laughed. "Thank goodness, we're all honest."

"Oh, right. I told them to check it."

Philip grinned like a kid who'd just gotten his way. "I'll come around seven o'clock. We'll go wherever you like."

Ellie smiled wide.

I finished her perm. A proper washing and styling, and she left with the soft, fluffy curls she wanted. I sat in the hairstylist chair and replayed the events in my mind. Somehow in a disaster involving neutralizer I'd ended up going out with the man I'd just broken up with. Whew! It seemed as long as Philip stayed in Triville he'd weasel his way into my life.

How about seeing each other as friends. If he agreed to no more hugging and kissing, that would work. He wouldn't get too lonely between now and when Mr. Jacobsen called, and seeing him wouldn't be as hard on my heart. He seemed oblivious to the pain our dating could cause, but surely he'd understand when I explained it.

9

Philip lay on his back on the bed with his hands clasped behind his head and gazed at the drab beige ceiling. The gloomy motel room matched his mood with the thick curtains shut tight and the lamp the only light turned on. He lived one day at a time taking care of whatever was right in front of him, but that wasn't working for Eve and him.

He couldn't count on getting his way as he did today. He needed to understand Eve's concerns and address them. He only got inside women's heads to figure out what they wanted in stock portfolios. This was so much more difficult, but he'd do it. Eve was worth it. The same restlessness and nerves-at-loose ends that plagued him in New York churned inside him without her in his life.

What motivated her to agree to go out with him again? Had he gotten that pitiable look he used to give his mom and dad as a teen when he wanted to take out the car? The same one Sarah Miles said he had when she agreed to partner with him in last year's doubles at The Village Tennis Club. Margaret Neely accused him of looking helpless when she agreed to join him for the company picnic. It was more a habit than intentional, but apparently, it worked every time.

He didn't want Eve to go out with him because of a pathetic expression. He wanted her to be happy with him. The mileage between them appeared to bother her most. Now that he'd stopped enjoying her company long enough to think about it, she was right. He didn't like it either. He'd fix it. He had plenty of free sky miles. He could fly to Merchantville, rent a car, and drive the one and a-half-hour trip to Triville every week-end.

He bounded off the bed and headed to the sink to brush his teeth. Mr. Jacobsen could spend the rest of the month with his daughter as long as George continued to allow him to work from Triville, and why wouldn't he? He wiped extra toothpaste off his face with the towel. This was the company's most important deal right now, and no one needed one of the seminars George sent him to conduct.

He proceeded to the shower stall whistling, the happy notes resounding over the splashing water. He got out and tugged on a pair of jeans and a shirt as soon as possible and left. He strolled outside into a mountain breeze cooling the warm evening and picked up his stride. In no time it seemed he was parking in front of Eve's house and zipping past the dogwood tree on the way to the door. A blue pick-up sat in the driveway.

Pete and Charlie had arrived.

Thank goodness, they were handling repairs after her appointments, staying out of her hair. He smiled at his pun. He hoped they'd finish soon. The shop meant so much to Eve. He pressed the doorbell, and she answered. "Hi gorgeous."

Her lips turned up slightly on the corners then broke into a big smile. "Hello. I'd like to stop by and see how Pete and Charlie are doing."

"Sure." He trekked to the shop with Eve, and they went inside.

"How's it going?" Eve asked.

Pete held a drywall board. Charlie finished nailing it, and they turned around. "We'll complete the putty tonight and sand it tomorrow," Pete said.

"I sure appreciate it." A hint of sadness lined Eve's tone.

Philip lowered his head. Had she hoped for more progress? If he could go back and not crash into Eve's shop, he would. But he probably wouldn't have met her then. Maybe he'd have the car stall in front of Eve's Clips, but he couldn't do either. What was done was done. He and Eve proceeded to the car. "Where to?"

"Anywhere." Eve's voice lacked warmth, sounded matter-of-fact.

Maybe she was tired. She worked awfully hard in Eve's Clips, and there'd been so much happening. "Have you eaten?"

"No. I just wasn't hungry earlier." Eve chuckled. "I'll think of a place that's not at the top of a hill."

At least she still had a sense of humor about the old car. Maybe she was loosening up.

She clicked her fingers. "The Fish Barn. They serve trout caught in the stream beside the restaurant. Do you like trout?"

"I'm a fish lover." She could have asked him if he liked nails, and he'd have said he did.

Eve leaned forward. "Turn right, and it'll be on the right."

Philip pulled into a dimly lit gravel lot in front of a rambling rustic, wooden building with a low roof and parked. The soft glow of the spotlight washed over trees, grass, and wildflowers lining the banks of the brook beside them. The cool, moist air from the clear-as-glass water tickled his nostrils as he helped Eve out of the car.

He put his arm around her waist, and the touch of her made his night sparkle on the way to the entrance. A hostess took them to a screened porch overlooking the river and laid paper menus on a picnic table. Philip couldn't help but stare at Eve, the most beautiful woman he'd ever seen.

"The special is fried trout with French fries or a baked potato plus grilled zucchini."

When had the waiter arrived? Philip directed his gaze toward him. "That sounds good. I'll go with the baked potato."

"I'll have the same," Eve said.

Philip searched her face. Was this the right moment to talk to her about visiting Triville after he finished his business here? The way his stomach knotted for wanting to get their relationship back on track he'd rather bring it up now than later. Then he could enjoy this much-discussed mountain trout. "I've been thinking about a plan to see you after I talk to Mr. Jacobsen and return home."

"Really? I'll be here, and you'll be in New York." She sounded distant, detached.

"I thought you'd be happy."

"Long distance relationships don't work very well, I've heard."

Philip's eye twitched. "How can you say that? I'm the one making an effort to ensure we see each other." His stomach churned. He should have waited until after they ate.

Eve practically climbed across the table, her wide eyes blazing. "You're the one leaving."

He sat back in his seat and gestured with his palm up. "But I don't live here." Of course, he'd leave, but he wouldn't cut her out of his life. He intended for their relationship to work. Why couldn't she understand that?

"Right. That's my point. Sometimes I think you simply don't look life square in the face."

"What does that mean?"

"You don't see things as they really are."

Surely she didn't think he'd move to Triville. He'd offered to work part-time from the motel after he saw Mr. Jacobsen, but other than servicing that one account there was nothing in Triville for him businesswise. They were at an impasse. "You still don't want to see me after tonight?" Sorrow choked him as he said the words, but he had to ask.

The waiter served two steaming plates with the aroma of fresh fish wafting from them.

Eve took hold of her fork and picked at the trout. "We could see each other as friends."

Philip wrinkled his brow. *What was she talking about?* "I thought we were friends already."

She twirled the fork in a circle, flakes of fish falling on her plate. "Yes, that's right, but we don't always act like friends."

Philip nearly bent double. She might as well have hit him in the stomach with a board. "I've tried to be a good friend to you. I thought I was."

"You've been the best of friends." Her lips quivered as though she might burst into tears.

Had he said something right or wrong? "OK. In what way have I not acted like a friend?"

Eve bit her bottom lip and cast her gaze down. "All that kissing and hugging."

His mouth flew open in shock. He snapped it shut. "I don't understand."

She looked up and glared at him. "It's just a bit too

much for someone I'm only going to see for a few more weeks."

Had she not heard a word he'd said? "Eve, that's what I'm telling you. I'm coming back to see you on the week-ends after I leave, and I'll work here part-time occasionally. Didn't you hear me?"

The people beside them and in front of them turned and stared. He hadn't realized he'd spoken so loudly.

The dark-haired man to their right scooted to the edge of his chair, leaned over, and smirked. "Yeah, lady, give the guy a chance!"

Diners around Eve and Philip focused their gazes directly at Eve.

The man turned to face the thin woman with him and mumbled. "Is she hard-hearted or what?"

She knitted her blonde eyebrows. "Shhh, Andy. It's none of your business."

Philip couldn't believe all the people eyeing Eve and him. "The guy's right. You have to give us a chance," he whispered.

Eve sat silent. Then she cracked a little smile. Had the man gotten to her?

"OK, we'll see each other as friends by my definition until you leave. If you come back on the week-ends, we'll see how it goes."

"Are you saying you don't trust me?"

"No, I don't trust myself."

She didn't trust herself with him? She didn't trust how she felt about him or their future? Whichever, he'd leave well enough alone. She would continue to see him. He was trying to get over being a spur-of-the-moment guy and think things through, but she needed to give him a break.

She smiled at him. "I'll look forward to the week-ends."

His word was good. His stomach settled down, and the trout melted in his mouth. Eve bit into her fish and scooped up bite after bite. Everything must be fine. "Thank you for suggesting this place."

"I'm glad you like it." She finished her baked potato.

"Dessert?"

"Oh, no. I'm stuffed."

"Me, too." Philip paid the waiter, and they meandered outside.

Crickets chirped breaking the silence of the still, quiet night as Philip and Eve got in the car. Philip headed toward the highway and then pulled onto the road leading to the shop, the damage he'd caused to it weighing heavy on his mind. Yet that was only part of Eve's problem. What was going on with those products? "I've been wondering how you ended up with faulty conditioner and why the neutralizer was missing from that box of stinky stuff. It seems a bit strange."

"Not the permanents. It happened before. The company said it was a slip-up at the factory. The person who was supposed to add neutralizer to the packages probably didn't do it."

"What about quality control?"

"I don't know much about production, but in this economy the company may have cut back," Eve said as they pulled into her driveway.

The work truck was gone. Pete and Charlie must have finished for the evening.

Eve glanced at the shop as they proceeded toward her front door. "I guess they'll show up tomorrow, at least for a while," she said as the key clicked in the lock.

Philip followed her inside.

She sat in the easy chair then pointed to the sofa. "Have a seat."

He raised his eyebrows. She wouldn't sit next to him. He settled there, but this distance was only temporary. He'd see to that. "How did you solve the missing neutralizer situation before?"

"I noticed it right away and had plenty of cash on hand. I was able to go to the drugstore while the solution set my client's curls. Later after I told the company about it, they sent me replacements for the kits I had on hand."

Apparently, an honest mistake. "What about the conditioner?" Philip asked.

"It's never happened before." She said the word never real loud. "Beauty supply products make my shop special. Generally speaking, people who aren't hairstylists can't purchase them. Having anything go wrong with them makes me as angry as a wet cat." She lowered her head. "I don't want to buy a bottle of conditioner and a permanent from the drugstore to have in an emergency, but I will."

"Good idea until we get to the bottom of this." Sleep called Philip and he stood. "We're not finished with your Just Right order yet."

Eve got up, but stayed on her side of the room until he headed toward the door.

He turned to her with the urge to kiss her filling his heart, but she stood back and waved. "Good night."

Would she ever let down her guard? He'd have to make sure she did. Where should he start to straighten out her product mess?

10

I shut the front door and pressed my back hard against the wood paneling. The grandfather clock ticking sounded loud in the quiet house and reminded me I was alone. Tears welled up as I trudged down the hall. I tried to push my sorrow back, hurried to the bedroom, and fell on top of the comforter.

How could sending Philip away without a kiss leave me so empty? I rubbed my hand on the other side of the bed and gazed at the place where Jordan once lay. Only a kid when I started dating him, I'd never gone out with anyone else until Philip. What did I know of people from New York? Logic told me I'd probably ruined this relationship asking to only be Philip's friend. How could I not ask with worry over losing someone else I cared for gnawing at me?

Other people like Ellie lost spouses and moved on. Of course her two-timing first husband used her. Made my blood boil to think about it, but she'd moved forward and found happiness with Smitty. Why couldn't I do that? It'd help if Philip lived here.

I forced myself off the bed and showered quickly. Weak from the upset I'd caused myself I donned my nightgown, crawled under the covers, and hoped sleep would cure me. I threw the comforter off. Was I foolish to push Philip away? Why did God send someone who lived in New York? The clock on the nightstand stared me in the face—three-thirty in the morning. Finally, exhaustion overtook me and I slept.

~*~

The alarm buzzing jarred me at eight o'clock. Sunlight danced on the light green leaves and pink blossoms on the mimosa tree in front of the window. Jordan loved the spring flowers. He had been such a gentle man. Philip seemed mild-mannered too. Would keeping a distance from Philip lessen the pain when he ran off to New York, or was my heart already bound to him?

I sat up and wiggled my feet into the white satin bedroom shoes Joyce Westmoreland had given me last Christmas. Oh, poor Joyce's hair. Nausea hit my stomach, but I swallowed it and trod to the kitchen.

Starting breakfast seemed such a chore, and could I even eat? Would Pete and Charlie show up? I needed strength for the day. I placed a piece of bread in the toaster and fresh grounds and water in the coffee maker. In no time it seemed my morning libation appeared in the glass pot, and the toast popped up. I sat at the pine table and stared at my breakfast.

Some people read tea leaves. Could anyone read coffee grounds? What would these say about Philip and me? Ellie thought the two of us had a chance at love, and I could be happy anywhere with the right person. The man in the restaurant probably was right. I needed to give Philip a chance.

What was I thinking? I'd told him not to call. It was done. I nibbled the food and sipped my drink then dressed in a pair of black pants and a white blouse and headed outside.

The sun kissed my arms as I trekked from the house to the shop. A fruity hairspray mixed with the odor of pungent permanent solution hit me in the face when I entered the building. *Whew.* I raised the new window then turned on the fan.

Seeing bare drywall and white putty specs on the floor probably should have encouraged me because it meant repairs were underway. Instead it triggered thoughts of what a disaster my shop and my life were. I went to the back, returned with the mop, and cleaned up the mess beside the window.

Mary Lou Moore and her mother, Loraine Peters, entered at ten-thirty.

As a kid Mary Lou rested on the floor in their den while Mrs. Peters sat on the sofa and brushed Mary Lou's long, dark hair. They stayed there for an hour or more, Mrs. Peters brushing and Mary Lou soaking up her mother's love. Mr. Peters, on the other hand, was abusive, often leaving welts and wounds on Mary Lou.

"Good morning, how nice to see both of you."

Mary Lou peered at the window. "I'm sorry about the accident."

"Thank you. Pete and Charlie will sand the putty today, but they'll stay out of our way. Who wants to go first?"

Mary Lou gestured toward her mom. "She will. Her best friend, Mrs. Green, is coming for lunch."

Mrs. Peters removed her red head scarf and touched her gray hair. "I washed it, so all you need to do is roll it, if you don't mind. The get together wasn't planned when I made the appointment." She gazed at me with searching blue eyes as though she feared I might be angry with her.

How silly. I couldn't be peeved at sweet Mrs.

Peters over something so trivial. Anyway, it probably was for the best considering my conditioner situation.

"That's perfectly fine." I patted the middle salon chair. "Have a seat. I'll have you out in no time."

I picked up the medium-sized rollers and wound one into her thin hair.

Mary Lou sat back as Pete and Charlie came in. "Mornin' Eve. Mary Lou, Mrs. Peters. We'll try not to disturb you," Pete said.

Charlie held up a big square of sandpaper and headed toward the drywall. "Just ignore us."

The two of them marched to the wall beside the window. Scratching permeated the room. Pete and Charlie picked up the pace to loud fast scraping, and my nerves vibrated. I rolled up Mrs. Peters' hair as quickly as possible, but she stared at me with annoyed blue eyes as I put her under the dryer.

The sanding grew more intense and wrinkles creased Mary Lou's brow.

"How's little Carrie doing?" I asked hoping to take her mind off the racket.

"She's getting such an attitude. That child will be spoiled rotten between Mama brushing her hair and James tickling her every night when he comes home."

Mary Lou had married James Moore, a lanky guy with sandy blond hair and blue eyes, ten years ago. If he'd ever raised his voice, let alone struck anyone, I'd never heard tell of it. Just the kind of man Mary Lou needed. "Sounds like Carrie has lots of admirers." Ahh, to hear of the joy a child could bring to others, but never know it for myself. A pain pricked my heart. "I'll get your mom out now."

"Poor thing. Her hair's so thin it doesn't take it any time to dry," Mary Lou said.

I always curled and combed Mrs. Peters' hair in a way that made it appear to have more volume. "She'll look pretty." I glanced over my shoulder and winked at Mary Lou as I lifted the dryer off Mrs. Peters' head. Mrs. Peters padded to the salon chair, and I put the finishing touches on her "'do." Then she and Mary Lou left.

I never thought I'd see the day I wanted to flee my shop, but I welcomed the drive to Smitty's. I hurried to the car, let the peace and quiet soak into my pores on the way there, and entered the drugstore.

I wanted to work through the repairs, but that irritating noise unraveled my nerves. I couldn't force it on my customers. I'd have to cancel the rest of my appointments for today, but I was glad that Mary Lou and Mrs. Peters had come. Mrs. Peters looked nice for her visit with Mrs. Green. To think about poor Mrs. Peters living with that monster all those years. She'd stayed with him until he died for a reason only she knew.

My wonderful Jordan was taken from me so soon. He was on his way to see his mother. He'd kissed me good-bye that morning and said, "I'll return." Now Philip told me he was going away, but he would come to visit. Why couldn't I believe he'd come back and wrap my heart around the joy he brought? Well, it was too late now.

I grabbed the conditioner from aisle three, checked out, and returned to the shop. Pete and Charlie had disappeared. They must've gone to lunch.

Having to resort to store brands because of the unpredictable Just Right supplies humiliated me. If I could I'd buy the most expensive stock for my customers. This solution to the product problem was neither permanent nor the one I preferred, but it temporarily restored my sense of control over my shop. With authority I set my purchase on the shelf behind the shampoo bowl and threw the bottle from Durbin in the trash.

Squares of sandpaper lay on the floor in the midst of putty dust. A small piece of typing paper stuck out from under Pete's toolbox. I picked it up. *Maybe you'd rather be DIE-ed red.* My stomach knotted.

This message sounded childlike, just as Philip had pointed out when he found the first two, but at the same time, this was sinister. Were the notes from the thieves who robbed the businesses in Merchantville? Did they plan to break into the beauty shop? I shivered inside as I laid the message on the desk. Even if Philip were right, I had to make the shop my top priority. My clients were my livelihood and my friends. I sat down and rescheduled the rest of today's customers with nausea swimming in my stomach over all the business I continued to lose.

Mary Lou entered, Pete and Charlie on her heels, the door slamming behind them.

She dropped down on the edge of the shampoo chair. "It means so much to Mama to get together with Charlene. You know, Charlene has that chronic fatigue syndrome. That's why they don't plan things ahead. She calls Mama when she feels up to coming."

"I understand."

I put a burgundy cape around Mary Lou's shoulders, clipped it shut in front, and leaned her back, giving a good shampoo and rinse. My hand jerked as I snatched up the conditioner. Was I cheating using a store brand? I had no choice if I wanted to give Mary Lou the fine hairdo she deserved. That's why I took things into my own hands and went to the drugstore. Not only that, another flood in the shop was more than I could stand, and Philip wasn't here to clean it up. A sinking sensation pulsed through my veins. How could he have made so much difference in my life in such a short time?

There I was thinking about him again. Four years of being alone, and I had to fall for some guy from New York. He might as well have been from the moon. The liquid dripped into my hand when I tilted the bottle.

I rubbed it into Mary Lou's hair. My heart accelerated as I squirted water on her locks. Silly. It worked fine. Why wouldn't it? I wrapped a towel around Mary Lou's head with my cheeks burning. Life was difficult enough without a bottle of conditioner making a nervous wreck out of a person. The next time Durbin called, he would have to straighten this out. I was a Just Right customer, even if I lived in the mountains miles from the city.

Mary Lou made a path across the gray laminate floor to the first salon chair and plunked down.

The sandpaper scratching in the background seemed louder near the styling station. I bristled. "What type hairdo would you like today?"

"I loved the way you fixed it last time, back over my ears with bangs brushed to the left. Just do that." Mary Lou didn't let on that the sanding bothered her, but how could it not?

I parted off her hair, held a section at an angle, and placed the razor at the end using short, choppy motions. Then I repeated the action.

"Who's the handsome guy you've been seeing?"

I quit cutting her hair as an ache filled my chest.

Would people ever stop asking about Philip? I might as well have rented a billboard with our names and photos.

Mary Lou must have sensed my dismay. She slipped her small, chubby hand out from under the cape and gestured. "I don't mean to be nosey. I'm happy for you. You're young and attractive. It's time you found somebody."

I hadn't found somebody. That was why I regarded her question as an intrusion instead of the caring inquiry she probably meant it to be. I resumed the trim. "He's just passing through town. It's nothing serious."

"Oh, I thought..."

The door opened, and Philip traipsed in. "Good morning, Eve, ma'am." He glanced at the men, but they had their backs to us and appeared to be entrenched in their work.

I was speechless.

Mary Lou was all smiles. "Oh, hi. I'm Mary Lou Moore. My husband, James, and I run the laundry and dry cleaners." She extended her hand to him, and he shook it.

"Nice to meet you, Mary Lou."

"Likewise. I saw you in Bob's Diner with Eve, but I'm glad to say hello to you in person."

No end to it. Could I disappear into thin air? Not only had Philip created more gossip by coming to the shop, but seeing him unleashed my frustration over our relationship, whether it was justified or not. I stopped cutting Mary Lou's hair and put my fist on my hip while still holding the razor. "What can I do for you?" I tried not to sound irritated, but I failed.

Mary Lou bit her bottom lip then glanced at him

and me as though she thought we were having a lover's spat. Were we?

He shifted his weight. "I ah, ah, wondered if Mr. Jacobsen had called yet."

"No, he hasn't. Looks like you're stuck in Triville a little while longer."

Mary Lou sucked in a deep breath.

Philip meandered over and stood beside me. "I feel privileged to be here."

Mary Lou exhaled.

I lifted the razor to cut her hair, but couldn't reach her head for Philip's arm. I glared at him and tightened my jaw.

He moved over, and I snipped. "Privileged, huh?"

"Yes, how about having a bite of lunch or dinner with me?"

Last night and this morning I was nearly sick because I thought I'd never hear from Philip again. Now he'd asked me out and my heart clenched tight with fear of caring more for him if I accepted. I'd remind him of our recent agreement and say I'd go as long as he kept a distance from me, but I hardly wanted to mention our personal business in front of Mary Lou.

She tapped Philip's arm. "I hear Bob's special tonight is Eve's favorite, pot roast. She wouldn't want to miss that." She shifted in her seat and gave me a harsh look as though she thought it would be unkind of me to decline. "Would you?"

Philip's eyebrows shot up. "Bob's Diner, it is. What time?"

"*Pff.* All right, dinner sounds fine. I can leave by seven."

"I'll pick you up then." Philip strolled out,

shutting the door quietly behind him, as if noise mattered with all the sanding.

There seemed to be no end to my customers' fascination with Philip. Did they see a future I didn't? Whether they did or not, Philip apparently knew how to win their hearts.

Maybe he cared about me and that's why he went to the trouble to arrange a date, or he could have been bored. Triville wasn't the most exciting town in the world. I ran the electric razor up Mary Lou's neck, blew her hair dry, and twirled it with the round brush to create soft curls around her face. "You look cute."

She stood. "Thank you. I love this." She handed me a cash payment then left.

No more clients today, but the books had to be balanced. I sat at the desk a couple feet from Pete and Charlie, the sandpaper scratching in the background as I pulled the ledger out of the middle drawer. The numbers looked pretty good. I could cover my bills. Durbin's supplies cost fifteen dollars more than what I'd paid Les Shepherd, the salesman he replaced. It was ironic that prices kept going up with people's earnings going down, at least it seemed that way for me. I thanked the Lord I had enough to live. Then I closed the desk drawer and stood. "See you later, Pete, Charlie."

"We're almost finished with the sanding. Want to pick out a paint color?" Pete asked.

"Oh, sure." The sooner the better.

Pete left and returned with small sample squares stuck on a large piece of paper and handed it to me. "We'll try to do this at night, so you can work during the day. You can turn on the air conditioner and raise the window to get rid of the fresh paint "aroma." Pete raised his blond eyebrows when he said the word aroma.

I chuckled. "Right. Well, I'll stick with a neutral color. The vanilla ice cream looks nice."

"You're quick. Lots of people take several days to decide." Pete rubbed his forehead. "I know you want it finished as soon as possible, but I recommend covering all the walls, because the new paint won't match the old. For that reason the insurance should pick up the tab for the entire job."

"I'll ask my agent to check to make sure, but yes, that sounds good."

"I'll give you a buzz when we have the paint. You can let us in or leave the key under the rock."

Pete returned to his sanding, and I headed for the house, a headache starting at my temples as I went through the doorway. I'd already missed so many appointments. When I'd styled Joyce's hair in spite of the disaster, I'd created a wretched mess. Today, I'd managed to give Mary Lou and Mrs. Peters' nice hairdos, but had to cancel everyone else. As soon as Pete and Charlie started painting either my customers would have to sit in the odor or I'd have to close. Would this ever end?

English sparrows flitted from the stoop as I crossed the yard and opened the door to the house. The quiet shouted at me, and loneliness echoed in the room. It would be good to go out.

I turned to the right, headed down the hall straight to the bedroom closet, and put my hand on a black dress with beads around the scooped neck. I pulled it back as though the garment burned it. No. Jordan gave me that outfit. It had been one of his favorites. Jordan lived in my mind, my heart, and every fiber, bone, and nerve in my body. How could I ever let go of him?

11

Following the outline of my lips I stood at the vanity and applied pink lipstick with a hint of violet.

The doorbell rang.

I set down the cosmetic, switched off the bathroom light, and proceeded to the foyer trying to grasp happiness for the rest of today. If only yesterday and tomorrow would stop getting in the way. I opened the door. "Hi."

Philip's mouth turned up on the corners as he escorted me to the car and let me in the passenger's seat. "You look stunning."

My heart danced. "Thank you."

He got in and sat silent until we approached the hill leading to Bob's Diner. "We'll see what she's made of."

The vehicle jerked and nearly stopped. Philip gave it more gas, and it chugged along then cut out again. He took a deep breath, restarted the engine, and floor-boarded it. The last surge took us to the parking lot where the road leveled off and the view from the top of the mountain took away a person's breath. He parked in a space near the door then sat back in his seat as though he needed to collect himself. "So, we're having pot roast tonight?"

Made my mouth water to think about it. "Yes. If you like roast beef, you'll love Bob's. It's the best."

He hopped out and sauntered around the car. His

silhouette cut into the twilight coming over the mountain, and he disappeared into the night. In the blink of an eye the passenger's door opened, and he was back.

I sucked in a tiny breath as I got out and wished it was a sign he'd keep showing up at my door. We waved and smiled at Ellie and Smitty as we meandered through locals in the parking lot on our way to the entrance.

Strange, the shop remained a disaster, my hairdos drove me nuts, and Philip was still from New York. But he was here now, and the same security I found with my favorite stuffed toy when I was young surrounded me.

Inside, townspeople scooted into the booths and sat on bar stools at the counter as customers passed one another in the aisle.

Bonnie Sue emerged from the kitchen carrying two steaming plates. "Comin' through."

I spotted a table for two in a corner in the back and led Philip to it.

He pulled out my chair and plopped down across from me. By then Bonnie Sue stood against his seat. "Why, hello, handsome. What can I get for ya'll tonight?"

It warmed my heart every time disinterest over Bonnie Sue's advances showed in Philip's eyes.

"Nice to see you again," he said.

He was such a gentleman, and a kind person. It was a wonder Bonnie Sue's grin didn't break her cheeks.

"We'll have the special, and I'll take a sweet tea?" He glanced at me.

"Yes, that sounds great."

"Comin' right up." Bonnie Sue smacked her chewing gum then smiled and batted her eyelashes at Philip before she left.

He thumped his fingers on the table. "We're far enough away from the noise to talk."

"Yep. Private dining at its best." I chuckled then remembered I wanted to tell Philip about the latest ominous message. "I found another note. This one said maybe I'd rather be DIE-ed red."

Philip put his forefinger on his lips. "I still believe it was a kid with nothing to do. Where was it?"

"Stuck under Pete's toolbox near the wall." Philip was probably right, but the threats buzzed in my head like pesky mosquitoes. "I try not to leave a large amount of money in the shop, but I imagine the hair blowers, combs, towels, capes, and supplies could be resold." My recent product disasters popped in my head. "Well, whoever bought the conditioner would be in for a frightful shock."

Philip chuckled.

I did too. "But seriously, just the thought of someone breaking in gives me the shivers."

Philip chewed his bottom lip. "A child probably wrote the menacing letters and somehow they ended up where you didn't notice them until the wreck disturbed everything."

"It's possible the air from the hair blowers and dryer blew the notes. They could've flown up and stuck on a drawer or piece of woodwork underneath the desk as you said. Then the crash would have knocked them loose."

"If I thought they were written by an adult, I'd tell you to report them to the police, but I don't think it's necessary."

The conviction in Philip's voice convinced me, and I erased worry over the scribbled threats from my mind.

In moments Bonnie Sue brought our plates, a tantalizing aroma floating from them. "Here ya' go. Enjoy."

"Thank you. That was quick," Philip said.

"We knew you were comin'." Bonnie Sue pranced off with a wiggle in her step.

Philip bit into his entrée. "My, my. I'm stuffing myself with another delicious meal. I hope I'm not gaining weight."

"You don't look any larger, but there's a free scale at Frank's General Store if you want to use it after we finish."

"What kind of place is Frank's?"

"It's Triville's answer to the grocery superstore."

"Oh, sure. Weighing there sounds like a good idea." Philip dug into his meal.

Apparently, the talk of putting on pounds hadn't put a damper on his appetite, and it shouldn't. He looked perfect.

He scooped up the last bite of his beef and rubbed his stomach. "On to the scale. Weighing will either make me stop eating as much, or I'll know I can keep it up."

Bonnie Sue appeared, her gaze focused on Philip. "Dessert?"

Philip's eyes grew wide. "Can people eat dessert after all of that?"

"Oh, sure, some of 'em can." Bonnie Sue smacked her chewing gum. "All right then, here's your check."

~*~

Philip picked up the bill and followed Eve. They wound through the clientele seated at the booths and tables to the cashier. Philip paid and they meandered outside. He couldn't believe he was going to weigh. A date with Eve was like unwrapping a present. There was no telling what might pop up.

He escorted her through the maze of people in the parking lot as she smiled or waved at nearly everyone before they scooted into the car. Then she gave him directions to a dimly lit, rustic, one-story building.

She leaned forward and peered out the windshield. "It's only eight forty-five. I think he's still open."

"OK. Rule number one. After eating so much I'm allowed to deduct three pounds. I'm bound to weigh more now than I will in the morning," Philip bounded out and opened Eve's door.

"That's permitted," she said. "You'll like this place. When Frank was a kid, during the summers he sat at a produce stand in front of their farmhouse and sold crops to tourists. He never enjoyed tilling the land, growing, or harvesting, but he loved selling. He arranged their fruits and veggies in tasteful designs." Enthusiasm rang from Eve's voice as they entered underneath a big sign that read Frank's Country Store. She motioned toward a bin of oranges. "See. His displays still look tempting."

Philip glanced at the arrangement and nodded. "Yeah. He sounds like an interesting guy." He stared at the oiled wooden floor. If he'd ever seen one he couldn't remember it.

Field greens, cabbages, carrots, and more veggies spanned the wall. Large containers of fresh flowers sat near the empty check-out lanes.

Clearing the canned and frozen goods, Eve dashed past tables of blue jeans and T-shirts to the tool section, and finally the pharmacy. The scale, which sat in a nook beside the counter for filling prescriptions, resembled those in doctors' offices except the weight unit across the top beam was much larger.

Eve motioned toward it. "Here we are. Hop up there."

Philip stood on the scale and moved the weight. Three hundred and fifty pounds. Was this thing defective? He must have done something wrong. He pushed the weight to the end and started over. Three hundred fifty pounds. "No way. I couldn't have gained that much."

Eve snickered.

He turned around and caught her an instant before she eased off. "I don't believe you did that."

She laughed out loud. She was full of fun.

Philip pulled her close, brushed the hair from her face and kissed her.

A door squeaked and Frank burst out of the storeroom. "Eve Castleberry, the two of you will have to find another place to..." He waved his large hand in their direction. "I'm going to lock up."

Heat crawled up Philip's neck. He felt like a kid who'd pulled a prank at church and gotten caught by the preacher.

Eve wiggled free and pointed her finger at him. "You're not supposed to be doing that anywhere, and certainly not in public. Frank, we were just..."

Frank laughed. "Oh, yeah, I see you were. As far as I'm concerned, it's about time, but not here."

Eve sputtered as bad as Lloyd's car. "No Frank,

we were, were...we came for Philip to weigh."

Frank tapped his foot and stared at them with a twinkle in his green eyes as though he enjoyed embarrassing Eve.

Eve tilted up her chin. "Have you met Philip?"

Frank stuck out his right hand.

Philip shook it. He'd never seen Eve at a loss for words. In spite of the awkward moment, a big grin formed inside him and spread across his face.

She put her hand on her hip. "This is hopeless. Goodnight, Frank."

"See ya', Eve. Don't worry. I won't tell anyone about your clandestine meeting at the scale in the back of my store."

Eve practically ran toward the front door.

Philip stayed on her heels, catching up to her in time to open the passenger door before he took his seat. "You're really upset aren't you? He was only teasing."

"That's easy for you to say. You don't live here. It won't matter to you if the whole town's talking about us. You're leaving."

Philip started the car and pulled out. Seemed like they couldn't do anything without Eve mentioning that he'd leave eventually. Why dwell on it? It wasn't the big deal she made it out to be. They'd still see each other. "He said he wouldn't gossip about us."

Tears welled up in Eve's eyes. "Wanna' bet?"

Philip turned the steering wheel, winding around a sharp curve. "Sweetheart, it's all right. We were just clowning around."

"So I'm only someone to clown around with? I'm not sure I even want to be friends."

Eve was such a wonderful person, but she couldn't

seem to relax and enjoy their time together no matter what Philip said or did. Was she hunting a reason not to care about him? Why couldn't she embrace their relationship? "You're twisting my words." Philip drove onto Main Street.

She sniffled. "There wasn't supposed to be anymore kissing and hugging. You broke your promise."

Philip pulled into Eve's driveway, the headlights shining on the bare wall where the bricks had fallen from around the beauty shop. He hoped she wouldn't get more upset looking at it. He cut the engine, grabbed her, and held her tight. He never wanted to let go, but finally he did then rubbed his hand around her back in circles. "How can I not kiss and hug you? You have that cute personality. You're beautiful, and I care so much about you."

She gazed at him with big doe eyes. Did she believe him?

He wanted Eve. He had to make her see the two of them would work.

12

My dressy shoes pinched my feet. I kicked them off, sank into the rocker in my bedroom and wiggled my toes on the carpet. The teachers' meeting for vacation Bible School signaled summer just around the corner. It wouldn't be long until I'd serve the children their snacks. I'd started volunteering to help after Jordan died, and I realized I'd never have kids of my own. I fingered a loose string on the cushion in the chair. Jordan and I had bought it to rock the babies we'd have. Tears pooled in my eyes.

My gaze fell on the message machine on the desk where Jordan once worked. Had Philip called? No blinking red light. Had it finally occurred to him our romance could go nowhere? I couldn't bear to date Philip and then lose him, but at the same time I wanted him to be happy. What a tangled web. Did I lack strength? It seemed everyone believed I should move on and find someone. Even Frank had said, "It's about time."

I bowed my head, told God how I felt, even though He already knew, asked for His help, and put the entire situation in His hands. *Amen.* If God wanted me to find someone, He would send him.

I headed to the kitchen to make coffee and turned on the faucet.

The phone rang.

"Hello?"

"Hi."

I held out the receiver and stared at it. Only seconds ago I'd explained to God how I couldn't continue this relationship with Philip. What a strange answer to my prayer. Had He not heard me? I'd thought in time He'd send someone who could work out things with me.

"Mr. Jacobsen called my room and wanted to know when I could meet with him. I've been tying up the loose ends on his portfolio."

"Wasn't he going to contact you at the shop?"

"Well, with only one motel in town and one on the outskirts, it wasn't difficult to find my phone number. We're meeting tomorrow. You could go with me since that's your day off."

How could Philip suggest we do anything together? I kept explaining how difficult it would be when he left. "I hope Pete and Charlie will paint then. If they do, I'll phone my customers scheduled for Tuesday and Wednesday to find out if they mind the odor, or if they'd like to keep their appointments."

"That's a good idea. You could contact them before we leave."

I tried with all the strength in me not to let Philip's invitation touch my heart, but it fluttered like a school girl's. "Actually Philip, when I didn't hear from you, I assumed you understood we shouldn't go out again."

"No such thing. I've been counting the hours until I could be with you."

"Sure, and a blonde and three bears are dancing outside my kitchen window."

"Come on. I still need to finish this portfolio then write a letter and a summary for George. I hope you'll go with me. Having you there will make it easier for me to talk to Mr. Jacobsen." He paused. "I'll come mop your shop floor again."

I couldn't help but laugh. He'd rescued me in the beauty parlor twice. Now he asked for my help. I couldn't say no. "All right, as long as we see Mr. Jacobsen, and you bring me straight home. Absolutely no kissing and hugging, and you can't use the scales to weigh anywhere."

Philip chuckled. "It's a deal. I'll pick you up at eleven-thirty."

"See you then." This was not the answer I'd expected to my prayer about dating Philip, but I made the coffee with my heart a little lighter just because I'd talked to him. A bright colored finch flitted by my window sharing its rare beauty for a moment. Then it flew away like the happiness that flitted in and out of my life. If only the joy could last.

~*~

Monday morning I sat at the table gulping down the last bite of breakfast as the doorbell rang right on time. I sprang up and answered.

Philip wore a navy pin-striped suit and a tie.

"You look so handsome, but Mr. Jacobsen's very casual."

He peered down at his pants then at me. "What do you suggest?"

"Shed the jacket and tie."

"We'll stop by the motel. See how important your

recommendations are. Do you know the way to Mr. Jacobsen's? The only address I found said Jacobsen Mountain."

"Yes. I'll navigate," I said as Philip let me in the car.

We drove to the Triville Motel, and I waited while he went in. White paint with tan trim and lush green holly bushes brightened the old building.

He returned wearing a pair of khaki pants and a black shirt that highlighted his dark hair. "Is this better?"

I drank in the brassy smell of his cologne as he scooted in the driver's seat. "Perfect. The aftershave's nice too."

He started the car and backed out. "Like that, huh? Which way?"

"Stay on the highway until we reach High Peak Road. Then turn left."

I recalled the scary route with hairpin turns. "Maybe we should have driven my car. I'm sorry I was running late and didn't think of it."

Philip patted the steering wheel. "She wouldn't let me down."

His optimism warmed my heart, but he'd never seen the narrow passageway. I'd traveled it when Mrs. Jacobsen held a luncheon at their house for Triville's high school graduates. A dirt bank dotted with pine trees flanked the road on the left. Scraggly trees grew as best they could in small amounts of dirt between the boulders in the steep cliff on the right. The recollection lay heavy on my mind, and I slumped. The vehicle rolled backward and jarred me.

Philip smiled and gunned the engine. The car lunged forward then backward again. He mashed the pedal to the floor. The old car bucked, the jerking action snapping back my head.

"How far?" Worry lined his voice.

"I'm not sure, but there's a sharp curve coming up." My hands started to sweat.

The rear of the car spun to the right. My heart leapt in my throat. Part of the back tire on the passenger's side stuck off the road over the bluff. I could hardly breathe.

"What's wrong?"

"We—we're—the tire." I swallowed. "If we move backward when you let off the brake, we'll go over." The words flew out in staccato rhythm.

Philip turned pale. "I'll gradually give it gas and release the brake slowly. Don't look down."

"Don't worry."

"I'll start in a second."

The hair on my arm stood on end. "OK." My voice sounded so weak I barely heard it. *Dear Lord, please help us.*

Philip's right foot lightly tapped the accelerator. The part of the passenger's rear wheel touching the road bounced on rocks and gravel at the edge of the cliff.

I'm going to die.

Philip mashed a little harder and turned into the curve. The tire came closer to the mountain.

I exhaled.

He gave the engine more gas and the edge of the wheel surged forward and touched solid ground with a thud.

I went as limp as the wet towels in my shop.

He pulled ahead, straightened the car, and inched up the steep grade.

Thank you, Lord. Amen. I pointed ahead with a shaky finger. "There it is."

"Thank goodness." Philip parked on the gravel drive, wiped the sweat off his forehead, and helped me out.

Stalwarts on the skyscape, the blue hills in the distance reached high as though they attempted to join Heaven. The sun danced on the tops shining a spotlight on their strength and majesty. Like God's firm, constant love for us, their steadfast grandeur never changed. I breathed the magnificence of His creation and my hands quit trembling.

Philip gazed at them with wide eyes. "This view is almost worth the scare."

He motioned for me to go first along a stone walkway to the brown, wood-frame house.

I brushed by a mountain laurel bush bursting with purple flowers beside the rock stoop.

Corley Jacobsen had lived here for as long as I could remember. He graduated from Harvard with a degree in business and economic management and met Martha Greenwood while he was there. She traveled in high society in Boston, Massachusetts. My dad used to say old Corley had something goin' none of us understood.

As far as I knew, Mr. Jacobsen never ascribed to Martha's social circles and remained a mountaineer in spirit. She often gave showers for brides-to-be as well as parties for Triville's teens. Mine was lovely. She'd served dainty star-shaped pimento cheese and chicken salad sandwiches, and tea cakes. While Mrs. Jacobsen entertained, shopped in New York, and vacationed overseas, Mr. Jacobsen ran a successful lumber business from this mountain.

Philip pressed the bell.

Mr. Jacobsen pulled the door back immediately as though he'd been watching for us. He remained lanky and fit, but his salt and pepper colored hair had turned white since the last time I'd seen him.

"Come in, come in." He greeted us with a raspy voice as we strolled into a spacious living room with a huge glass window overlooking the hills. He adjusted the straps on his overalls then extended his right hand with large blood vessels showing underneath thin skin.

Philip shook it.

"How you doin', son?"

"Fine. I appreciate your seeing me today."

"Not a problem." Mr. Jacobsen rubbed the white stubble on his chin. "If my Martha was here, she'd offer you some tea or coffee. In her honor, that's what I'll do. I've already brewed a pot of coffee. I figured a man wants a hearty drink, but when you said the missy was coming, I thought she might like tea." He grinned a toothy smile at me. "I have that too."

He waved his arm for us to follow him to a large kitchen with brown granite counter tops and an oak trestle table. "Sit down here, missy." He pulled out a chair facing a large window overlooking the mountainside. "Do you want the tea? It has a hint of peppermint."

Either was fine with me, but it appeared he'd gone to some trouble to make sure he had a special drink for our visit. Too, I imagined Martha used to drink it. "That would be lovely, Mr. Jacobsen. Could I help you fix it?"

He shook his head. "No, no. You and Mr. Wells—"

Philip put up his hand. "Please call me Philip."

"All right, Philip, you sit right there." He pointed

to a chair beside me then reached in a cupboard at the end of the counter and brought out a blue flowered creamer and sugar bowl. Taking slow steps that made me think he had arthritis, he went to the microwave and put in a cup. It dinged and he pulled out the hot water, stuck a tea bag in it, and set it on the table. Then he served coffee for Philip and him.

Hazelnut and peppermint aromas gave the kitchen a cozy ambiance. The window let the outside in, and the sun-streaked azaleas, dogwoods, and mountains in the distance poured their splendor into the room.

Mr. Jacobsen scooted up to the table across from Philip. "Son, how's this investment going to work?"

Philip pulled papers from his briefcase and spread them out. "In this economy I'm a strong believer in a little gold and silver. For diversity I've researched a few bonds and mutual funds I think will hold their own. All of this is in addition to your core blue chip stocks."

Philip's voice sounded strained and much too formal for Mr. Jacobsen's mountaineer spirit, but he peered at Philip with a twinkle in his eyes as though he saw something in him he liked.

Mr. Jacobsen laid his hand on the table. "Now, that's a good idea about gold and silver. Count me in with that. Leave those papers about the other stuff here. I'll call and let you know. But, you can take ah, say, one million right now and invest one-fourth in gold and the rest in silver. I'll get the money as soon as we're through visiting."

Philip gulped and set down his cup. "Get it?"

"Yeah, it's out back in the freezer."

Philip looked as though he'd seen a purple elephant with six legs, but only for an instant.

This didn't surprise me a bit.

Mr. Jacobsen either didn't notice Philip's shocked expression, or didn't let on he did. "How's that coffee, son? It'll grow hair on your chest, won't it?"

Sounded like my tea had been a good choice.

Philip looked Mr. Jacobsen right in the eyes. "I can feel the hair growing already." He sipped the last of his coffee.

Mr. Jacobsen slapped his knee, threw his head back, and his laugh boomed out loud.

Philip smiled. "I'll take good care of your investment."

"I know you will, son." Mr. Jacobsen pushed back his chair and headed toward a small sun porch off the kitchen.

We joined him as he touched a white wrought iron table. "Martha loved that thing. She used to sit there for hours and look out the glass wall."

My breath hitched in awe of this view of the massive towering mountains. Immovable and indestructible in this changing world. "I can see why."

"Yeah. I don't come out here anymore except to get out a steak or a hot dog. If I stay and sit, in my mind I see her across from me." His blue eyes grew misty.

"I understand," I said it softly.

"Ahh. I bet you do. You got a raw deal with Jordan dying so young. If nobody else can relate to my pain, I bet you can."

Philip's eyes snapped wide.

Mr. Jacobsen trudged to a freezer and opened the lid. "It's underneath these packages." He leaned over and pushed several ice cream cartons and steaks aside. "I'll count them off in hundreds for you. That way your bags won't weigh too much."

Philip sucked in air as he whirled around and looked back at the trestle table where he'd left his briefcase.

Mr. Jacobsen followed his gaze. "Son, I don't believe we can get it all in there. I'll be right back."

Philip grasped my hand and pulled me toward the kitchen. "We'll wait in here."

"You can if you want too. I'm not worried about you takin' any of it. It's too cold." Mr. Jacobsen chuckled. "Naw, I have a way of knowin' people I can trust. Anyway, you want to invest it not steal it. Eve's a God-fearin' church person. She wouldn't lay a hand on it."

"I appreciate your trust in us, but I'd feel better if I wait in here."

"That's fine." Mr. Jacobsen passed through the living room to the foyer and out of view.

Philip and I stood beside the glass-top stove, our used coffee cups and saucers sitting on the granite counter next to it.

"Jordan?"

This wasn't the place. "I'll tell you later."

"No. Who was he?"

"If you must know this instant, he was my husband."

Philip gasped then his eyes filled with compassion. "I'm sorry. How long were you married?"

"Ten years. We knew each other our entire lives. We started dating in tenth grade and married after I finished my cosmetology course." Thank goodness, the lump in my throat stayed put.

"I understand now why we can only be friends."

"No. That's not it. I believe Jordan would like for

us to go out."

"Why do you think that?"

"He'd want me to be happy."

"Then what's wrong?"

"You know. We live seven hundred miles apart."

"Eve, I've told you..."

Mr. Jacobsen's footsteps sounded nearby.

"You're right. We'll talk about this later."

Mr. Jacobsen appeared with one small duffle bag hanging from each arm and continued to the porch with us following.

He gave Philip an empty carrying case and reached his long arm through the frost hovering around the top of the freezer. He brought up several stacks of bills and handed them to Philip. "This is cold, hard cash, son." He rubbed his hands together and snickered at his joke.

We laughed too.

Philip turned toward the small white table and set down the sack. Mr. Jacobsen filled another.

Philip grasped one in each hand and trod toward the front door. The weight of them made his arms appear a couple inches longer than they usually looked. His mind probably stretched even further, considering how this money transfer differed from those usually made in New York.

"Let me know when you have my gold and silver investments. In the meantime I'll read those papers. You can come up again, and we'll talk." He winked at me. "Bring missy with you."

I touched him on the arm. "Thank you for the tea. I enjoyed my visit."

Philip walked straight to the car, set the cash on the gravel drive while he opened the trunk, and then hoisted it in.

I let myself into the passenger's side and gazed at Mr. Jacobsen standing in the doorway peering at us. As he'd said, we shared a bond of sorrow, he and I. Had he risen above his and forgiven life for what it did to him? Or, did life close in on him like a straitjacket and keep him from reaching out for joy?

Philip went back, said something to him, and shook his hand. Then he returned, got in the car, and poked his head out the window. "Thanks for the coffee and everything," he hollered toward the house.

Mr. Jacobsen moved outdoors, stood on the stoop, and waved as we pulled away.

I returned his gesture until he and the azaleas and dogwood trees disappeared. He had to be awfully lonely on the mountain without Martha. But then, no matter where we were, we were all isolated unless someone loved us.

Philip clenched his jaw. "I'm scared to death something will happen to that currency. People don't drive around with a million dollars. We'll get robbed."

"Who would break into a car that looks like this?"

"Yeah, you're probably right. I hadn't considered that. At least it's a smooth ride down the mountain." He relaxed his hold on the wheel. "Everyone in Triville will be talking about this."

"How will they know?"

"Beats me. I don't understand how the population of Triville gathers information. Is there some sort of network, or do residents pick up people's words like radio signals as they drift through the air?"

I couldn't help but chuckle. "No one knows about the money but you, Mr. Jacobsen, and me. He hardly ever comes off that mountain, and I certainly don't think he talks about the bills he keeps in the freezer when he does. I won't tell, and you won't, so how could anyone find out?"

"Everybody here knows everything."

"That's true."

"I'll book a flight to New York as soon as I return to the motel and take this investment to a bank."

"We have one."

"It's not a five-star institution. I have to be very careful with Mr. Jacobsen's cash until I make his purchases."

"You're a good businessman, Philip. You know people too. If you'd told Mr. Jacobsen he had to put the money in any bank, including yours, he wouldn't have done it. He doesn't trust them."

Philip pulled into my driveway. "The freezer was my clue." He reached over and hugged me tight. "Thanks for going with me. I'm staying with these bills until I deposit them tomorrow. If you don't mind, I'd rather not leave the car until I go back to the motel room and take the cash inside." He cast his gaze down. "I want to hear about Jordan, and I want to discuss us. I'll return as soon as possible, and we'll talk then."

I wasn't sure if he looked guilty because he wasn't walking me to the door, or because we weren't discussing Jordan, but I was fine with both. "I understand."

"Thanks."

I got out of the car, and Philip backed out. Sure, he'd return this time. He wasn't the kind of man to leave Lloyd's car sitting at the airport in Merchantville, but how many more times after this would he come back? A cloud of sadness surrounded me.

At least Pete and Charlie had come. I entered the

shop and turned on the light. Wow! I loved the vanilla ice cream walls. Alice Newberry had said she wanted to come no matter what. I looked forward to fixing her hair, but would it be enough to take my mind off Philip? Whatever would I do when he left for good?

13

Tuesday morning the alarm jarred me. I slapped the button and knocked the clock over. "No need to scare a person half out of her wits." My voice sounded as tired as I felt. I'd tossed and turned so much my comforter looked as if it'd been in the spin cycle in the washer. If only I'd told Philip to call when he arrived in New York.

He was a smart man and a quick thinker. He'd only acted without reason that one time when he slogged through all those suds in the beauty shop. Well, also when we went to see Mr. Jacobsen, he didn't seem to realize the road was hazardous, but since he'd never been there, he didn't know that. Would he see disaster coming?

I crawled out of bed, dressed in a pair of black pants and a white blouse, went to the kitchen, and cranked up the coffee pot. The drops falling into the glass container cut into the quiet morning, a hazelnut aroma wafting while I made toast. Finally, I poured a cup, sat down at the table, and munched breakfast.

I'd never been to New York, but I'd seen pictures of the city. In my mind's eye I watched Philip lug those two duffle bags down a busy street toward a bank. I shivered. He might not even make it into the building before someone mugged him.

I snatched a key from the hook beside the refrigerator and headed outdoors. The sun warmed my shoulders as I unlocked the shop, but the cheeriness of the day failed to follow me indoors. I entered and the strong paint odor insulted my nostrils. Following Pete's suggestion, I turned on the air conditioning and opened the window. Hoping to freshen the room before Alice arrived, I also mopped with pine-scented detergent.

Alice entered, her powder blue eyes twinkling. "Good morning."

Her blonde hair had grown out of shape and unruly around the sides of her face. Thick bangs puffed over her forehead nearly to her eyebrows.

"Hi, I'm airing out the place as best I can."

She waved her hand back and forth. "It's fine. I've waited too long to come in. I'm just glad to get my hair fixed."

Alice's husband, Jimbo, was a friendly, good old boy, but Alice, who'd made the dean's list at Duke, was the brains behind their law firm. She was also a great mom to their twin teenaged girls. She had little time for beauty shop appointments.

She inched down in the chair in front of the shampoo bowl and I draped a burgundy cape around her. I started scrubbing her hair, and she shut her eyes as though the shampooing relaxed her. She didn't open them until I finished and raised her up.

She pulled on a tendril. "I really need a cut. I've wanted to get in here for three weeks."

"I hear you. I'll have you all pretty again in no time," I said as she sank into the middle salon chair.

I parted off her locks and started clipping.

"Have you been dating someone? I'm in the office so much I don't keep up with my friends as I should, but Ellie Ringgold mentioned seeing you in Bob's

Diner with a guy."

My day wouldn't be complete if someone didn't ask about Philip. "I've been showing the sights to a man from New York. Nothing serious." Discussing Philip triggered thoughts of the danger he faced in New York with all that cash, and nausea hit me.

Her lips turned down. "I hoped it was."

"He'll leave soon. I'll probably never see him again."

"Oh, I'm sorry. I thought maybe..." Alice stopped in mid-sentence. "Why look at that. This hairdo's shaping up already. You've only finished the bangs, haven't even gotten to the sides yet."

I was thankful she changed the subject. My head spun with everyone pushing me to enter a relationship with Philip. Too bad they couldn't break the chains life had locked around my heart when Jordan died. Even when I tried to put the sorrow behind me and think about Philip, my brain short-circuited. One second I was nervous because I hadn't heard from him. The next instant anxiety rattled me because I dreaded him leaving Triville for good. "I'm glad you like it." I twirled the chair around and gave her the hand mirror. "There."

"You're a blessing."

I laughed, but her words sent warmth through me like a hug from one of the kids in Vacation Bible School. "I'm just a hairstylist."

"You're a talent." Alice stood and handed me her payment. "See you in a month before I look like one of those little, ungroomed Shih-tsu dogs."

I still grinned over Alice's comment about the canine as my neighbor, Ralph Wisner, entered.

He took big strides with his lanky legs to the first

styling station and dropped down into the chair. He worked fifty miles away in the Mountaineer Paper Mill, but he also raised chickens. If I was up at five o'clock in the morning and the world was quiet, I heard him in the coop. "Here chickee, chickee, chickee." As long as I'd known him, he'd liked birds. I had to give him credit though. He'd lived there for twelve years. So far not one chicken had gotten loose and ended up in my yard.

"How's it goin,' Ralph?"

He rubbed his hand across the top of his head. "Jane raves about a blond-haired model who advertises men's deodorant on television. After twenty years of marriage, I don't know what she's doing looking at some man on TV, but I thought if you had time, you could dye my hair the same color as his."

"Sure. If you don't mind the paint odor in here, I'll do it now."

Ralph peered at the walls. "Looks nice. No, it won't bother me. I'll smooth out the tangles." He leaned up, pulled a red comb from his back jeans pocket, and ran it through his hair.

I lowered the chair to allow for Ralph's height then touched him on the shoulder and handed him the color swatches. "Show me which one you want, and it's yours."

He flashed me a wide smile then eyed the samples. "That's it." Excitement rang in his voice.

I studied it for a moment. Confidence I could duplicate it exactly rippled over my skin. "I'll mix a special formula for you."

"Just so my hair turns out like that." He pointed to his selection.

"It will." I patted him on the shoulder then went to

the supply cabinet and searched the products on the second shelf. Seeing the boxes triggered thoughts of Philip putting them up for me. My muscles tightened. He had to be all right. Why didn't he call? Didn't he know I was getting more frantic over his situation every hour? I mixed the dye and developer, shook them in the application bottle, and returned to Ralph.

He relaxed his thin shoulders and sat back in the chair as I parted off his hair. Starting at the roots, I applied the dye. The strong scent mixed with the paint odor made my head throb. He gazed in the mirror with a fascinated look as though I was creating a work of art.

"The way I see it, I didn't need to drive thirty miles to the city to have my hair dyed. Everybody knows you're just as good, maybe better than those uptown hairstylists, and you're right next door."

Working in the foul odor just grew worthwhile. "Why, thank you."

"You're welcome."

I finished dying Ralph's thin hair quickly and fished a motorcycle magazine off the vanity for him. "You might enjoy this while you wait."

"Thanks." His lips turned up slightly as he clasped the periodical and leaned back in his chair.

I set the timer then swept up the clippings from Alice's haircut and straightened the combs and brushes.

Buzzing in fifteen minutes signaled blond for Ralph. I tapped him on the arm, and his eyes sparkled as though he couldn't wait to see the new look.

"I'm ready to rinse your hair."

He laid down the magazine, bounded to the shampoo bowl, and leaned back. The warm water I ran through his hair trickled onto my arm as I glanced at his head. Red? Suddenly my spirits fell. I turned up the spigot and flooded his hair as I worked my fingers through the strands. Fire engine red.

The nozzle swirled in the sink as I grabbed up the shampoo bottle, poured a little in my hand, and rubbed it into Ralph's mane, washing it again. Rinsing it, I held the sprayer close to his head. The clear liquid pulsated through his hair until the suds disappeared. Red. My hands shook as I turned off the faucet. "Ralph, I'll be right back."

He rose up and stuck out his long neck. "Is something wrong?"

"I don't think so." Even though I never would've ordered a bright red dye, I trekked across the room and checked the color of the formula I'd used. Thank goodness, I didn't accidentally do anything wrong. "No Ralph, we're in good shape. I'll give you another shampoo."

"Whatever you say." He leaned back.

I scrubbed so hard I worried I might irritate Ralph's scalp, but he lay as still as a rock. It was as though he'd endure anything to look like the man Jane admired so much. I raised him up, and my knees nearly buckled. "Ralph, this isn't the shade I mixed, but I..."

"What are you saying?" His face turned white.

"I'm so sorry. I don't know what happened." I couldn't keep my voice from cracking.

He jumped up, threw off the cape, and stared in the mirror above the shampoo bowl. His lips trembled. His eyes widened, and he blew through his nose like a bull.

My heart pounded against my ribs as I yanked up

the shampoo and conditioner bottles from the shelf behind the shampoo bowl. Taking ragged breaths I grabbed the towels and capes and held them against my chest. "I'll dye it again for nothing. I promise I'll fix it like you want."

He glared at me.

Would Ralph hit me? I shook inside.

"I think you've done quite enough." He stomped out of the shop, the door slamming behind him.

My headache pounded. Too dizzy to stand, I sank into the chair at my desk. I couldn't hold back the tears cascading down my cheeks. I must've cried for an hour before I wiped them and picked up the receiver to my landline.

"Hi Janet, this is Eve Castleberry, I'm so sorry, but I'm really sick."

"Yeah. You sound all stopped up. I hope you get better soon. Could I come next Tuesday?"

The disappointment lining Janet's voice rubbed against my nerves like the sandpaper Pete and Charlie used. Logically, I should have written her into my appointment book. I had to make a living. Right now though, I couldn't take one more thing going wrong. What if I ruined her hair, or rather, my products did? It'd gotten to the point where I'd rather pick up a snake than one of my supplies, and snakes gave me the willies. "My head hurts so bad I can't see the schedule." If I closed the shop now, at least I'd save my reputation and my friends. "Uh, Janet, I'll be closing Eve's Clips."

"Oh, until you feel better. OK, we'll talk then."

I didn't have the energy to clarify or argue, so I said nothing. I hung up then informed my other customers the shop would shut down permanently.

They'd tell Janet and everyone else in town by midnight. Nonetheless, I'd put out a "closed" sign tomorrow. I locked up and sobbed, my shoulders shaking all the way to the house.

The foyer and hall seemed miles long as I trod down them to the bedroom, my mind in a fog. The comforter swirled as I fell onto it. My head pounded, and my heart ached. I had nothing.

The phone ringing exacerbated the pain.

I reached out, searching for the receiver on the wicker nightstand. "Hello."

"Hi, are you all right?"

"Philip!" I sat up in bed, propped the pillow behind me, and wiped my tears. He was safe. Relief at hearing his voice raced through my bones. I'd already lost one man dear to me. I might lose Philip to New York, but he was alive. Joy spurted from my heart in spite of the pain in it over my shop. "Uh, I'm having a bit of a problem at the shop, but I'm OK. How about you?"

"I'm having a disaster." He sounded disheartened.

"I knew carting those duffle bags to a bank in New York would tempt a robber. When I didn't hear from you, I was afraid you'd been mugged."

"Ohhh, the citizens of New York had nothing to do with it. I deplaned carrying the luggage. A cab picked me up right outside the main entrance to the airport and drove me straight home. I waltzed inside and unzipped the satchels in the living room. Guess what? They were stuffed with toilet paper. The cash is gone." Horror filled Philip's voice.

"How can that be? No one except you, me, and Mr. Jacobsen knew you had it."

"I have no idea, but I will soon. I'm catching the

first plane back to Merchantville. Then I'm coming to Triville to trace my steps and find the money."

"What will you tell your boss? Don't you have to account for an investor's funds, especially if they're missing?"

"Technically, yes, every penny, but I intend to locate the currency before George learns what happened."

I put my hands over my mouth. How long could Philip hide the facts? "That's good, I suppose. Aren't you taking a risk keeping the theft a secret?"

"As of right now, as far as I know the bills disappeared thirty minutes ago. That's when I first noticed I didn't have them. Shoot, I could've misplaced them."

Was Philip with his one-track mind making sense, or was my head hurting so bad I couldn't think straight?

"If something goes wrong, and I can't retrieve the money soon, I'll report the theft, but I have to give myself a chance." Philip's voice broke up. "You will help me figure this out, won't you? I need to know I can count on you."

Poor Philip. "Of course, I'll do whatever I can. Triville has a police department with a chief and one other officer. Then there's Thad."

"We may end up at the police station, but I hope not. I'd rather the town of Triville not discuss Mr. Jacobsen's money over their morning coffee. If he thinks I'm irresponsible, he'll yank his account."

Now, he convinced me. "You might find it quickly if you devise a good plan."

"So, what's happening in the shop?"

Tears sprang to my eyes, and I sniffled. I explained

about Ralph and how I'd told my customers not to come for their appointments.

"That makes me furious, but affirms my suspicions. Something's wrong with your products. When I return, we'll take care of that too."

I blew my nose. "All right, Philip."

"Please don't worry about the money or the shop. Do you need to use dye tomorrow?"

I couldn't help but cry. "I told you. I'm closing Eve's Clips."

"No, you said you made cancellations. Sweetheart, don't do that. I know how much that place means to you."

How could he possibly know? I'd never told him I lived for the shop now that Jordan was gone. Philip was so intelligent.

"Are you all right?" The concern in his voice filtered through the phone.

"I'm as good as can be expected." I was numb, and didn't know much of anything, including the answer to his question. I didn't want to upset him though.

"I wish I were there."

That's what I'd been trying to tell him. "See. That's what I'm talkin' about. You're not."

"I know. We have lots to discuss. I still want to hear about Jordan—"

How could I tell him about Jordan? He'd never understand. He was speaking, but I hadn't heard a word since he said Jordan's name. "What, Philip? What were you saying?"

"Sweetheart, I want to talk about us. I miss you very much, and I've only been gone twenty-four hours. We'll see each other a lot. Trust me."

"I do trust you, Philip. I just don't know how we

can see each other with you in New York and me in Triville."

"The planes still fly between New York and Merchantville. That's only an hour-and-a-half from Triville. It'll work. You'll see, but first I need to get Mr. Jacobsen's money and solve your problem. Whew. I'm exhausted. A few hours of sleep might go a long way toward helping me think clearly. The last thing I want to do when I return is fall asleep while driving and wreck the car."

His shaky voice worried me. "Right. The car's enough of a wreck as it is. Take a nap. When you get here, I'll be around. I won't be working."

"Don't close the shop. Since you've already called some people, go ahead and put the sign out, but just for tomorrow."

Apparently he was so preoccupied with Mr. Jacobsen's money he didn't understand I'd already shut down the shop. "I'll see you when you get here."

"Good night. I'm sending you a hug and kiss."

"You too, Philip." I hung up and rolled over in bed. Philip and I were only two people. How could we solve all these problems?

14

Philip paced back and forth between the huge panoramic window and the mahogany coffee table in his New York penthouse. Outside the itinerate preachers, celebrities, successful businessmen, thieves, muggers, and murderers filled the streets, but he lost a million dollars in a tiny town in the North Carolina mountains. His nerves never had vibrated under his skin before, but they did now.

He breezed past his business and economics books organized alphabetically by authors in the mahogany bookcase on his way to the kitchen. Priscilla, the maid, always left this place sparkling. His copper pans shone like new pennies above the island.

He reached in the cabinet, all the glasses turned upside down and lined up taller to shorter. He filled one. Water squirted on the brown granite counter top. He'd stained Priscilla's perfect kitchen. The water would evaporate. He no longer cared about a showcase condo or the events that required he have one. He had to leave and get back Mr. Jacobsen's money, or his dream for Eve and him would fly away with a mountain breeze.

If only she were here. He depended on her. Who would've thought someone from New York would require help navigating a town as small as Triville? In New York he needed to know the streets, but in Triville he had to understand the folks. Eve introduced him to the residents and more importantly, showed him how to interact with them. She understood those who lived in the community as well as the ways of mountaineers in general. He could depend on her to know what he'd overlooked that led to the theft.

He missed the smell of her hair and the feel of her soft cheek. He couldn't help but chuckle about the scale at Frank's. He wandered into the bedroom, and the lemon oil Priscilla used wafted from the mahogany computer center.

The sooner he solved this problem the sooner he could work things out with Eve. He pulled out his keyboard and clicked the keys to find the earliest flight. Finally, he booked one out of LaGuardia at six o'clock in the morning. He'd have to wake up at four, but he itched all over for wanting to return to Triville and find the money. He showered and fell into bed with the muscles in his legs twitching. Finally his eyelids grew heavy, his nerves settled, and he dozed off.

He sat at a walnut desk and tapped his computer keys. The phone interrupted him.

"Hi, can you meet me at Bob's Diner?"

"Sure, Eve. I'm on my way?"

He locked the office, left, drove up the hill lined with green, leafy oak trees to the restaurant and sat at a booth. Eve came in, looking gorgeous in a black dress.

Bonnie Sue sashayed over, popping her chewing gum. "What ya'll gonna' have?"

The alarm sounded and Philip sat straight up. He placed his feet on the beige carpet and rubbed his head. Were there enough people in those mountains to warrant an office? Make More Money didn't have a branch in Western North Carolina.

Put on anything. Just get out of here and find that cash. He wouldn't be working from any city if he didn't. He grabbed a green shirt, tugged on a pair of khaki pants, and hurried out.

Inside the elevator, he tapped his foot until finally it stopped. He charged across the marble floor in the lobby and raced outside. In seconds brakes squealed as a yellow taxi halted. The cabbie lifted his cap and scratched his head. "Hop in, buddy."

Philip scooted in the backseat.

"Where to?" The driver spoke over his shoulder.

"LaGuardia."

"I shoulda' known, this time a morning.' It's a good hour to go, though. We shouldn't have any traffic tie-ups."

"Great." Philip rubbed his hands over his knees as if the action would relieve his anxiety. He hoped the cabbie was right.

Within thirty minutes the driver exited onto the road leading to the terminal. Six guys picked up orange cones blocking one lane. Two empty dump trucks pulled away followed by two rollers and a paving machine. Philip's heartbeat accelerated. Would he make his flight with the taxi creeping behind a construction crew?

As if he read Philip's mind, the driver said, "The flame's out in the paver's propane burner. Looks like those guys just finished. We'll zip around the NYC Airporter buses, cars and other vehicles." The driver motored past a truck and several vans and stopped at the entrance. "I brought you here at a good rate. Just add the surcharge."

"Here ya' go. Keep the change." Philip handed him extra, grabbed the duffle bags, and shut the cab door.

If only he could breeze through security and check his carry-on. Inside a line of people waiting for plastic boxes moved like giant snails in sock feet. Philip's hand shook for wanting to hurry as he snatched up a container and dropped in his loafers and keys. He shifted his weight back and forth to keep his nerves in tact while he watched the luggage bump in slow motion across the conveyor belt. He took a sigh of relief when he finally approached the end of the counter, but he stopped short and stared at his belongings before he snatched them. They lay piled on top of each other like the crisis in his life.

He shoved on his shoes and sprinted down the concourse to find the aircraft already boarding. He claimed his spot next to a blue-haired lady who pulled a needle and thread through a square piece of cloth.

"Hello." Her voice dripped with sweetness.

"Hi, ma'am."

Soon the jet taxied to the runway and took off, the trees turning to specs below then disappearing as they flew into a blue sky. At last, Philip had the quiet time he needed to recall his steps after he received Mr. Jaccobsen's money.

He'd left Mr. Jaccobsen's porch and put the bags in the car.

"I'm on my way to see my new grandbaby."

Philip's mind flip-flopped from the million dollars. "How nice, ma'am." He might as well try to make the lady comfortable. He pointed to her stitchery. "What are you sewing? My mother used to create those things."

Her thin lips stretched nearly across her face as she looked up. "It's a cross-stitch picture for the baby's room." She held it up. "See. It's a giraffe."

There. That should have put her at ease. He faced straight ahead, scooted as far over in his seat as he could, and started his recollection again.

He and Eve left Mr. Jacobsen's house. Then he put the bags in the trunk.

The lady moved the image up higher and closer to his face.

"Uh, yes ma'am, it's very cute."

Where was he? Oh, right.

He drove straight down the mountain to Eve's house. He hadn't even gotten out of the car to walk her to the door.

"It's a boy. They're naming him Ronald, and will call him Ronnie. I thought about making the giraffe blue, but I didn't want little Ronnie to grow up thinking giraffes were blue."

"Yes, ma'am. I think you made the right decision." *Please lady, stop talking so I can think.* Philip put his head in his hands.

"Oh, dear, are you all right? I'll call the stewardess."

He raised his head quickly. "No thank you, I'm fine."

"You look a little pale. How about a soda?"

"No ma'am, I don't need the stewardess." Philip gritted his teeth.

"Ronnie's older brother plays soccer, the goalie, I think. Did you ever play soccer?"

Philip's stomach knotted and hurt. "No, ma'am."

"I do worry about Junior. It's a rough game, isn't it?"

"I don't hear of too many young soccer players getting seriously hurt, but I don't know much about the sport."

She lowered her head.

Hallelujah.

She looked up. "I see." She commenced to tell Philip about Junior and Ronnie's sister, Suzy.

He gave up thinking about the money and nodded politely.

"We're approaching Merchantville." The pilot's voice drifted over the intercom.

The lady touched him on the arm. "We're almost there. This has been a lovely trip. I've enjoyed talking with you so much."

Philip took a deep breath. "Thank you, ma'am. I hope you have fun with Ronnie."

She chuckled. "Oooh, I'm sure I will."

At last the aircraft descended, landed, and rumbled to a stop. Philip bounded out of his seat. He put his hand on the overhead compartment.

The lady stood.

"Can I get something for you?"

"What a nice boy. Yes. I have a light blue cloth bag, fairly small."

Philip searched the luggage. "Is this it?"

The woman grasped it. "Thank you. Now you have a nice time doing—Um, what are you doing?"

If she only knew. "Just visiting."

He deplaned behind her, blew past the congested baggage claim, and practically ran through the doorway into the parking deck. He located the vehicle, threw in the duffle bags, and scooted in the driver's seat.

The urge to speed to Eve's Clips raced through his veins as the old car rumbled just under the expressway's sixty-five-mile per hour limit. Finally, he arrived and his heart danced as he parked and cut the engine. How could this seem more like home than his New York condo? Looked like Pete and Charlie had started brickwork on the outside of the building. Odd, no other cars were here.

He walked to the door. Peeping around a CLOSED sign through a crack in the drawn curtain, he knocked.

Eve slumped in the middle salon chair. The hair blowers lay idle on the vanity beside the combs and brushes.

He banged as hard as he could. "It's Philip."

Eve sat as still as a statue.

What was wrong? Did she not hear him pounding on the door? He pummeled it with his fist. He'd knock the door down if he had to.

Finally, she rose and let him in.

The sadness filling her eyes pierced his heart. He hugged her tight. Even with the missing money looming over his head, an urgency to make things right for her flooded his veins. "Sweetheart, what are you doing sitting in the dark?"

"Remember, I had to close."

"I thought that was temporary because you were upset over the dye."

"It's hopeless. It's one thing going wrong after another. I don't want to give up my shop. It's my life, but I care too much about my customers to keep ruining their hair. I'll lose more than clients. They're my friends. I doubt I have a buddy left in Triville." Tears rolled down Eve's cheeks.

Philip wiped one away. If only he could brush away all the trouble in Eve's life. Surely he could solve the supply problem. "Ahh, no, that's not true."

She sniffled. "I haven't heard from anyone since I closed. They don't want to come here, or they'd be calling."

"They're respecting your wishes."

"I never thought of it that way, but if I were one of them I'd contact me."

Philip sat down in the chair in front of the dryer and pulled Eve onto his lap. He put both arms around her waist. "Everybody's different. We can't expect other people to do what we would because they aren't us."

"They know I live alone. Seems like they'd wonder whether or not I'm all right."

"Like Lloyd said when he insisted I take the car, people in Triville take care of each other."

Eve broke out in sobs. "I haven't taken very good care of anybody. You should see poor Ralph. He was so excited about the new hair color."

"We'll straighten this out. People haven't contacted you yet, because it's only been—how long has it been?"

"I dyed his hair fire engine red yesterday."

"See, people don't even know you're closed."

"I told my customers scheduled for yesterday afternoon and today."

"They think you're not feeling well. Open the shop, call them, and reschedule. They'll flock in here, just as before." Philip's eyes felt like they had sand in them. "I think my lack of sleep and quick trips are getting to me."

Eve wiped her tears, reached up, and stroked Philip's cheek. "I'm sorry. Here I am talking about my clients, and you have a huge problem."

Warmth raced through Philip's veins. He wanted to give Eve a long, passionate kiss, but he couldn't because of her rules.

"You're so nice to suggest I re-open, but I can't do it. I no longer have the heart or strength to deal with products messing up my customers' hair."

"You shouldn't have to deal with them, and you won't. We'll fix this, but first let's find a good meal."

"How can I even think of food? My life is destroyed."

Eve was the most wonderful woman Philip had ever met, but no matter how many times he told her he planned to see her after he completed his business with Mr. Jacobsen, she seemed to ignore his words. "Sometimes I think you don't listen to anything I say."

She ran her fingers through his hair. "I listen." She gazed at him with sad, puppy dog eyes.

He held her tight. "It'll be all right. I promise. We'll chart a course of action, but let's feed you first. Just the two of us at a nice restaurant." He brushed her hair off her forehead. She was too nice a person to say it, but his crash caused some of her problems. Still, there was something very strange about those products. He had to help.

She stood. "All right, Philip. I'll change. You can wait in the shop or the house."

"If it's all right, I'll stay here and borrow a sheet of paper and pencil from your desk."

"Sure, make yourself at home. I'll be right back."

He had to straighten out the product situation, and then figure out who did what with the missing million dollars. Eve knew everyone in Triville, and she seemed to have an extra sense when it came to people. He didn't want to investigate without her, follow the wrong path, and waste time. He sat at Eve's desk and picked up the pen. How could he sort things out?

He tore a piece of paper off a pad, turned it

sideways, and put three headings on it, Mr. Jacobsen's money, Eve's products, and The Two of Us. He rested the end of the pen on his cheek. Should he tell Eve about his pipe dream of living in Triville? A smile bubbled inside him.

15

Philip couldn't believe he'd feel at home working in a room with pink flowered curtains, a shampoo bowl, and a hair dryer, but he did. He folded the paper he'd made notes on and shoved it in his pants pocket as Eve opened the shop door. She sauntered across the floor with her lips turned up slightly.

Seeing a hint of the Eve he'd known when he left sent a tingle up his spine. "Where to, gorgeous?" He stood.

"If you want the trout, that's good for me. I've never been to the Fish Barn for lunch."

"Sounds great." He wouldn't have to floorboard the gas pedal to drive up the side of a mountain. He put his arm around her waist and escorted her outside, warm sunshine and a refreshing mountain breeze stroking his cheeks as he helped her in the car. A good meal in a relaxing atmosphere should cure her malaise. The Eve he'd known before he left Triville would emerge and together they could handle anything— couldn't they? He slid in and started the engine.

Eve gazed out the window all the way to the restaurant, only turning her head toward him when he parked beside the river. He let her out and led her inside the rustic plank building. The host seated them on the screened porch, and they ordered two trout dinners with baked potatoes and sweet tea.

Again Eve focused out, peering through the huge

glass casement overlooking the forest. The sun sparkled like diamonds on the clear water and played off the trees and underbrush. Was she seeking the peacefulness the views in these hills usually brought?

If only he could find it too. But that was impossible with Eve so upset, and Mr. Jacobsen's money who knew where. He sat with his hands folded while his insides trembled. His heart pounded for wanting to tell Eve to snap out of the doldrums. He couldn't though. He cared too much about her. If he could stay patient everything would work out.

She finally faced him. "I'm sorry. I've been so upset I didn't ask about your flight back. Was it OK?"

"It was all right. I sat beside a grandmother and listened about a baby the parents plan to call Ronnie." He'd make conversation now, let her eat something. Then as soon as she finished they'd get to work. He had a plan to remedy her supply situation quickly. Then they could find Mr. Jacobsen's cash.

The waiter brought the meal, and Eve lit into it as though she hadn't eaten in a week. She held her fork in mid-air, a distant look in her dark eyes. "Was that an awkward conversation for you?"

It'd been stressful because he was trying to come up with a way to retrieve the money, but he liked grandmothers and kids. "Not really. Grandma did all the talking."

Eve laughed and color returned to her cheeks. Would she face their problems and help him locate the thief before Mr. Jacobsen or anyone else knew his investment was gone? He'd have to tell George within the next three or four days, but surely they could recover it before then. After all, Triville was a tiny town. He ate a bite of fish then sat back and listened to the babbling stream.

Eve peered around the room. "I like the table arrangement. The customers aren't sitting on top of each other." She sipped her tea.

"That's true." He tried to ignore her rambling detachment, immerse himself in the serenity, and wait for the right moment to bring her back to reality. Yet his mind raced like an old ticker tape imprinted with missing money...botched hairdos...empty duffle bags.... "I want to discuss something."

Eve propped her elbows on the table and placed her chin on top of her fists. "Can't we just enjoy our time together?"

His smart, perceptive Eve drifted while he sat on a bomb about to explode. "We have. Now we should get to work." Philip pushed his plate aside and leaned forward. "It's too confusing to think about your products and the money at the same time." Philip grinned. "One-track mind, you know. First up— opening your shop tomorrow."

Eve's eyes grew misty.

He couldn't stand the despair that seemed to have taken hold of her. "Don't be sad. I have a solution, at least a temporary one."

She sat up straight and wiped her right eye with her knuckle. "What?"

"We'll test all your merchandise and replace any faulty products with drugstore brands."

Eve's eyes widened. "Such a big job will take too long. What about Mr. Jacobsen's money?"

"With both of us working we'll have your products squared away in no time. Then we'll locate Mr. Jacobsen's funds together."

"Let's think of a strategy to recover the missing

bills right now." Eve ate the rest of her potato and laid down her napkin.

"As soon as you reschedule your customers, we'll start."

The waiter brought the bill and Philip paid.

He whisked Eve out of the restaurant and into the car and glanced at his watch. They'd only spent thirty minutes in the Fish Barn. He drove as fast as he could. No worries about getting a ticket. It wouldn't reach speeds that high. He parked in front of Eve's Clips. The entire outing—one hour and fifteen minutes. Plenty of time left.

Eve sprang out of the car and charged through the doorway of the shop.

Philip followed and caught up to her as she headed into the storage area.

"I think the shampoo's fine. Should we test it too?" Urgency filled her voice. His Eve was back.

"Yep. Every single bottle." Philip dashed to the supplies and scooped up as many containers of shampoo, dye, permanents, and conditioner as he could carry.

Eve grabbed the rest.

She lined up the bottles and boxes and turned the water on in the shampoo bowl. The sprayer flopped around and squirted the sides as her anxious eyes met Philip's.

"I'll hand you the shampoo," he said.

"Thanks." She poured a little in her hand, picked up the nozzle, and ran water over it.

Next Philip passed her a container of conditioner. She emptied some of the liquid in the sink and sprayed it with water. Suds swam in the shampoo bowl and anger lined Eve's eyes. She snatched up three more bottles. "It's a good thing I have the drugstore brand."

Philip tapped her arm. "Let's throw out the rest lest we have bubbles crawling all over the floor again."

She started laughing. "You're right. Hand over the dye."

Hope surged through Philip at Eve's happy outburst. "Chestnut Brown," he called out as he gave her a packet.

She squirted some on her hand and stuck it under the water. Red. "I don't believe this." She dropped the nozzle in the sink, opened another product, and wet it. "Red. Are they all red?"

"I don't think we're talking green." Philip gave the rest of them to her one by one. They all turned out red. This test was a good thing. They could quickly remedy Eve's situation then put all their effort into finding Mr. Jacobsen's cash.

"Bring the permanents to the vanity if you don't mind." Disgust lined her tone. Her shoulders slumped as she opened each box and found no neutralizer. "What's happening at the Just Right Company?"

Philip shook his head. "You should call them, but first make a list of the items you need from the drugstore. We'll buy them."

Eve stared at him with wide eyes.

"How many permanents? How much conditioner? What colors of dye?" Philip eased into the seat with the pink flowered cushion at the desk and grabbed a clean piece of paper and a pen.

She bit her bottom lip. "No matter the circumstances, I believe in integrity. I closed the shop because I could no longer bear to ruin my clients' hair. It broke my heart, but it was the right thing to do. Getting Eve's Clips open again means so much to me, but I don't know how my customers would feel if they knew I bought the conditioner, permanents, and dyes from the drugstore. They could do that themselves."

"Sweetheart, they're paying for the wonderful hairdos you create not the supplies you use."

Eve's eyes lit up. "Do you really believe that?"

"I know it."

"Ten permanents, twelve bottles of conditioner. Just write down "dye." It'll remind me to find the colors I need." She rolled her eyes. "As if I could forget."

Philip wrote frantically then laid down the pen and picked up the list.

She grabbed hold of it. "Thank you. I'll buy these and pick up more later if I need to. Go deal with the missing money. I'm sorry this distracted you."

He couldn't imagine attempting the investigation without Eve's perception and knowledge of the people of Triville. "I want you with me from the beginning. I'm going with you to the drugstore."

She hugged him tight. "Thank you. I'll hurry."

"How about a kiss." He puckered up. "Just a little one."

She gave him a peck on his lips. He wanted to hold her close and kiss her deep, but this wasn't the time. He guided her out the door.

She wrung her hands until they parked in front of the glass display window at the drugstore. He followed her as she tore inside, zipped to the hair products, and pulled what she needed off the shelves. Boxes and bottles bulged from her arms. "I didn't get a cart. Can you carry these?"

She looked so cute, and more importantly, happy. "Sure." He took a few items, dashed off for a basket, and swung the plastic container back and forth until he returned. They plunked the supplies in it and marched to check-out.

Mandy bounded from her stool as Eve placed her merchandise on the tall counter. She picked up a bottle of conditioner and her blue eyes widened. "Why are you buying all of these?"

"Business is booming." Philip leaned across Eve and wiggled his dark brows.

"You'll have to plan better next month." Mandy reached for a permanent box.

Philip rolled his eyes. "Is there something wrong with the products in this drugstore?"

Mandy stopped scanning and blinked. "No, why would you ask?"

"You don't seem to think they're good enough for Eve to use."

Mandy put her hand on her hip. "It isn't that. People expect a hair stylist to have special items from a supplier." Mandy jerked her head to one side. "I've never thought about whether they're better or not. It's just the way it is."

Eve looked as though someone had slapped her.

Philip placed the last permanent on the counter. "When someone's as talented as Eve, it doesn't matter where she buys her supplies."

The muscles in Mandy's face relaxed and she grinned. "That's true. Everybody knows that." She finished the transaction. "Thank you. Come again."

"Thanks. I will," Eve scooped up her purchase and they left.

Philip parked in Eve's driveway and checked his watch. In a little less than two hours they'd temporarily solved Eve's problem. She could phone her customers and start rolling up hair again.

Whoever had Mr. Jacobsen's bills would probably check them with a black light for marks. More than likely, Mr. Jacobsen would have used a rubber stamp or brush to personalize them with special ink. When the thieves realized that, they'd delay spending any of the money for a while. There were so few people in Triville. It couldn't take long to figure out which ones would steal. Once Eve stopped worrying about her shampoo, conditioner, and such, she'd have the presence of mind to think about who might be a thief. She could probably name them.

She knew everything about everyone from working in the shop so long. He'd give her another twenty minutes or so to get in touch with her clients. "I'm going to the motel to shower. When I return, we'll find Mr. Jacobsen's money."

16

I opened the door to the shop, but instead of rushing in to get ready for my first customer as I usually did, I hesitated. How dead the place seemed. The hair blowers, combs, and brushes on the vanity, the towels and burgundy capes stacked on the shelf above the shampoo bowl were useless without customers. But for Philip's help, it might've stayed this way.

I twirled the chair at the middle hairstylist station to liven up the room. Then I sat at my desk and pulled my appointment book from the drawer. I ran my hand over the top of it, flipped it open, and punched Janet's number in the phone.

"Hi, this is Eve Castleberry."

"Why, hello, I hope you're calling to reschedule my appointment. I don't want to go anywhere else."

How easy was that? "Yes. Is sometime tomorrow good?"

"Ten o'clock."

I recorded the hour. "See you then."

I hung up the receiver then contacted the rest. I'd have to work late on Friday and Saturday nights to accommodate them, but that was fine with me. I shut the book, patted it, and stood.

My hand trembled as I transferred shampoo and conditioner from the store-bought bottles into clear, unmarked containers above the shampoo bowl. Was I deceiving my customers? But they'd probably prefer store brands to wild, crazy hairdos. Monday morning I intended to call Just Right and get to the bottom of this chemical disaster.

If it weren't for Philip, I'd have no customers. My heart overflowed with warmth for him. "He's a fine man." There, I said it out loud. What would Jordan think about Philip? I shivered. My mind knew Jordan was gone, but he lived in my heart. I'd never stop loving him. How could I even think of having a relationship with someone else? I was fine before Philip crashed into my shop, wasn't I? Or had I been too numb to know I wasn't? I gritted my teeth at the way my emotions were driving me nuts. Then I caught a glimpse of my frustration in the mirror.

I recalled the day Jordan and I centered it in the shop. He'd climbed to the top rung of a ladder and stretched his slender frame over the vanity to put my new looking glass in place. "All right, I'll secure it now."

I'd asked him to move it up then to the left and the right, and he'd obliged. I'd finally said it looked perfect, and he'd mumbled, "We wouldn't want anything less." I'd laughed.

He'd worked so hard so I could have the shop. He wouldn't want me to give it up, but that's exactly what I planned to do until Philip changed my mind.

Big trouble waited if we didn't find that money, and I wanted to help Philip. For one thing, my sense of gratitude told me I owed him, but was there more? Pain started to throb around my temples for the upsetting circumstances in our lives.

I charged out of the shop to the house, hiked to the shower, and let the warm water soothe my nerves.

Who would do such a thing? Names rolled through my head as water splashed around me. None of them were thieves. I stepped out and dressed in a pair of jeans with a dark green T-shirt then put on my sneakers. The only thing I knew to do was tell Robert Grimes, the Chief of Police. The doorbell rang, and I bounded down the hall to answer.

"Hi." Sadness lined Philip's voice. I couldn't bear to see him so unhappy. He hugged me tight as if he needed someone to hold onto. Supporting him now, not letting him down mattered more to me than anything had since Jordan died. I squeezed him and he laid his head on my shoulder.

He released me and rubbed his forehead. "We have so many things to discuss. I want to hear all about Jordan, and I want to talk about us, but I have to find Mr. Jacobsen's money."

Hearing him say Jordan's name made me go limp inside, but I cared about Philip, and he was right about finding the missing cash. "I understand. Do you have a plan?"

We went to the den, and he sat on the sofa.

"All of my dreams are wrapped up in Mr. Jacobsen's account. If I'm successful servicing it, I'll build from it and start an office." His gaze met mine. "Grab a piece of paper. We'll write down every move I made after Mr. Jacobsen handed me the investment. Then we need to get started. I can only delay telling George a day or two."

I snatched a legal pad and pen and dropped down next to Philip.

"Begin with me carrying the duffle bags out of Mr. Jacobsen's house. I hoisted them into the trunk of the car."

I wrote that down.

"I drove you home then went straight to the motel, made my flight arrangements, and left for the airport. The bags stayed with me as my carry-on."

I laid down the pen. "You must've put them in the overhead compartment. Could someone on the plane have switched them?"

"No. I would have seen anyone who reached above me."

"OK. We need to back up. Could anyone have followed us to Mr. Jacobsen's, and then tailed you to the motel and airport?"

"Are you kidding? On that goat path."

I couldn't help but snicker. "You're right. We made it with the Lord's help, and only one car at a time can navigate the drive up his mountain." The money seemed accounted for every second, but clearly it hadn't been. "Maybe someone snooped around your motel room. Did you look inside the bags before leaving?"

Philip's eyes widened.. "No, why would I?"

I shook my head. "You're right. If you stayed right with them as you did on the way to the motel, no one could've bothered them. Did you leave them on the bed and go to the bathroom?"

The color drained from Philip's cheeks. "Oh, no." He slapped his forehead. "I guess someone could have watched my room, but who, and why? How did they get a key?"

"I don't know. Everybody in town realizes you're here to land Mr. Jacobsen's account." I couldn't believe anyone in Triville would stoop this low, but obviously someone had. "Try not to worry. Mr. Jacobsen rarely leaves his mountain to come to Triville. He had enough steak, burgers, and hot dogs in that freezer to last one person a year. We'll observe people and listen closely. Somebody will give away a clue when we least expect it."

"What people? Where?" Urgency lined Philip's tone.

"Everybody we see. Two of the best places to hear gossip are Bob's Diner and my beauty shop."

Philip patted his hair. "It's such a mess. It needs to be dyed and styled. I'll probably have to stay at your shop all day tomorrow."

I laughed, balled up my fist, and gave him a gentle tap on his biceps. "Oh, you. I'll take care of questioning my customers, and they won't even know I'm investigating a crime."

"Can you fix hair and listen at the same time?"

He had no idea. "That should be a requirement for graduating from cosmetology school. I'm part hairstylist, part psychologist, and part teacher." Attempting to lighten Philip's spirits, I chuckled. "And now, I'll be part detective."

"I knew you'd help." He hugged me and checked his watch. "Let's go to Bob's Diner tonight. I'll pick you up at seven."

"Sounds good."

Philip left.

When he was here, I wanted to be with him. Now, the room seemed empty. This would be my life when he returned to New York. How could I ever love Philip if I still loved Jordan? I wanted to scream.

~*~

Philip and I sat in one of the booths up front at Bob's as an old rock and roll song blared through the restaurant.

Bonnie Sue elbowed her way past a group of people waiting for the bus boy to clean a table. "How ya'll doin'?" She looked at Philip.

"We're fine, Bonnie Sue, but the music's a little loud." I wanted it lowered to facilitate my undercover surveillance. With the pressure of trying to solve this crime in only a few days hanging over us, the noise irritated my nerves like fingernails on a blackboard. I could hardly think.

"I guess I could turn it down a bit. You want to do a little sweet talkin',' don't cha'?" She eyed Philip. "I don't blame you."

"Just wanting to save my ears. We'll have a couple chili cheeseburgers with French fries and salads."

"Comin' right up." Bonnie Sue strutted off.

Philip put his elbows on the table and propped his chin in his hands. "There are so many people jammed in here. I don't know which one to listen to."

"We'll figure it out."

Lloyd moseyed over to us. "How's it goin'? Are Pete and Charlie finished with your shop?"

"They're through inside, and that's a load off my mind."

Philip reached out and shook Lloyd's hand. "Nice to see you."

"I should have that car part next week. I'll have yer' rental fixed in a day or two after it arrives. I guess you've about finished your business with Mr. Jacobsen."

Philip stiffened in his seat. "Uh, I, uh..."

I waved my hand in the air. "He likes it here. He'll

be around." Lloyd was blocking my view of people filing inside. My nerves danced.

"I see. I figured Philip was wondering about that part, but I guess he has other things on his mind." He rubbed his hands on his pants. "I came in from work to pick up a to-go order. I wanted to say hello, but I better head out."

I pulled a napkin out of the holder and laid it in front of Philip. "Thanks for coming over."

"You bet. See ya' later." Lloyd meandered toward the take-out counter.

Philip knitted his brows. "Why does he think I've finished my business?"

"Probably just making conversation or worrying that he might be holding you up."

Bonnie Sue set down our drinks. "Two sweet teas. Your food's right behind 'em." She left and returned with two steaming plates. "Enjoy."

"Thanks, Bonnie Sue," Philip spoke in staccato rhythm.

"You're welcome, handsome." She held her head high and put a wiggle in her walk as she headed back to the kitchen.

Philip leaned over the table without bumping into his food. "Do you think Lloyd had anything to do with the theft?"

His words charged through me like an electrical current. People didn't come any better than Lloyd, but then Philip hadn't lived his whole life in Triville. "No. Lloyd's a good ole' boy." I lowered my voice. "It's getting crowded. Customers waiting for a seat will jam in here. Eat slowly and eavesdrop."

Philip nodded then bit into his burger. "This is so good."

"Uh-huh."

Two guys I'd never seen wandered in. One was redheaded; the other, a blond. They wore jeans, black T-shirts, and motorcycle boots. Could've been passing through.

Philip stopped eating and peered at the men.

I tapped the table.

"What is it?"

"Don't stare at them."

"I'm not very good at this." He poured ketchup over his French fries.

"It's OK. Keep listening."

We sat silent as we nibbled dinner, first gazing at our plates then glancing around.

The redheaded man moved closer to the blond. "So, you're going to acquire what's left of the fortune, huh. How much is it?" He spoke under his breath out the side of his mouth.

The blond shrugged. "I'm not sure after the lawyer invests some of the money with a fancy firm in New York, but there's plenty to go around."

Philip's eyes snapped wide.

"How are you going to convince him to give it to you?" The redheaded man touched the blond guy's shoulder.

"I'll pay him a visit and ask him to turn over my share. If that doesn't work, I'll take other measures."

The redhead curled his lips into a crooked grin. "What are you thinking? Legal or illegal?"

Bonnie Sue brushed by carrying a plate of fried chicken. "Hey guys, there's a seat in the back if you want it."

The suspicious-sounding men headed for the table Bonnie Sue pointed out.

Philip gulped. "They were talking about Mr. Jacobsen. I'm sitting right here until they leave and then we'll follow them."

"It sounded as though one of them thinks he's entitled to money from an estate, and he's determined to get it legally or illegally. He might steal cash given the opportunity."

"Those creeps don't even live here do they?" Disgust rang in Philip's tone.

"You're better at this than you think. You've stayed in Triville less than a month, and you picked out two strangers."

"I met you two weeks ago tomorrow." He ran his hand lightly over my fingers. "I feel as though I've known you forever."

I probably should have told Philip it seemed that way for me too, but I couldn't commit my doubting, fearful heart to someone passing through town. Frustration at my complicated life irritated my skin like alcohol on a scrape. "I guess I'm growing on you just as Reverend Binder said."

Philip held his burger in midair. "To say the least. But back to eavesdropping. I'm almost finished with dinner, but I'd like to stay and observe those two if it's all right with you."

"Oh, sure."

Bonnie Sue pranced by the table and peered at our empty plates. Then she returned and picked them up. "Ya'll want anything else?"

"Yes, if you don't mind, we'd like two cups of coffee and…" Philip glanced at me.

"Can't beat Bob's apple cobbler."

"Apple cobbler, it is."

Bonnie Sue winked at Philip. "Comin' right up."

In moments Bonnie Sue served the dessert.

Philip tasted his. "Yum."

The contented look that flickered in his eyes told me how much he liked it, but in moments he focused a hard stare toward the back of the restaurant.

I shoved in the last of my cobbler and hoped those strangers would accommodate us. Sure enough, the dudes clomped past our table.

Philip snatched up the bill and flew out of his seat.

I sprang up and followed.

"Do you have a quarter?" Philip peered at me.

I grabbed one from my coin purse and handed it to him.

"This is the right amount." He laid it on the counter beside the register and charged out the door.

The two men trudged toward a white pick-up.

Philip practically ran to the old car. He helped me into the passenger's seat, scooted in the driver's side, and started the engine.

In moments, the truck motor roared, and they backed out.

Philip wheeled in behind them.

The guys drove through town and pulled onto the expressway. The light on the surface street right before the freeway exit turned red, but Philip kept his speed.

"Stop, there's a policeman."

He beat the steering wheel. "I can't."

"Either you'll stop now, or he'll pull you over. Those creeps will be back. We'll see them again."

Philip gritted his teeth and put on his brakes until the old vehicle halted. "I can't believe there's a cop out here. What makes you think they'll return?"

"They're hanging around here for a reason."

"What could it be?"

"I don't know, but they'll be back."

"I'll be ready. If only I could have tailed them tonight and gotten the cash." Philip hit the steering wheel with the palm of his hand. "I don't have forever."

"I know, but look on the positive side. We've made great strides, and we have tomorrow."

17

I stuck my head out from under the sheet in the dimly lit bedroom. What was I thinking booking Angel Epps at seven-thirty this morning before she went to Eileen's Department Store? I threw back the comforter and crawled out of bed. Forcing my tired body to move, I tugged on a pair of black pants and a white blouse.

Half asleep, I wandered to the kitchen, filled the coffee maker, and switched it on. Then I dropped a piece of bread in the toaster. The brown liquid dripping in the clear pot blended with the clock, ticking away Philip's time to find the thieves and to stay in Triville.

I yearned to help Philip make things right for Mr. Jacobsen's account, even though he'd flee Triville as soon as he did. The toast popped up and my mouth watered. I grabbed it and slathered it with butter and jelly, poured my coffee, and ate. I had to be strong when Philip left and not let life crush me the way it had when Jordan died. I cleaned up the table and headed to the salon.

Cool mountain air whipped around the corner of the house and ruffled the azaleas Jordan had planted as I opened the shop door. The dreariness of the room with no lights turned on and the sun not yet bright enough to shine through the window slapped me in the face. I quickly flipped the switch and the ceiling and vanity lights blinked the first signs of life.

"Good morning, Eve."

I flinched and spun around.

"I hope you didn't mind getting up this early to cut my hair." Angel came through the doorway.

"Not at all. Let's wash it first." I moved over to the shampoo bowl and patted it, and she dropped down into the seat.

I fastened a burgundy cape around her and turned on the spigot. By the time the water thumped through the plumbing and I'd finished my routine, the coffee had kicked in, and I was awake.

Angel marched to the middle styling station and plunked down.

"What's happening early in the morning at Eileen's?" I parted off sections of her hair.

"I'm a manager now in Women's Clothing. Come by. I'll help you find something to wear next time you go out with that handsome guy you've been seeing." Her lips stretched into a smile. "Philip, right?"

Rather than explain our temporary relationship, I went along with the idea of us dating. "Why, thank you. Yes, it's Philip. And congratulations on your promotion." I finished her cut and blew her hair dry.

She paid and started to leave, but stopped at the door and turned around. "I wasn't kidding about that good looking outfit. Philip's quite the talk of the town. The other day in the drugstore I heard two total strangers discussing him and Mr. Jacobsen."

I couldn't stop my eyebrows from shooting up as my ears opened wide. Were they the same guys Philip and I saw? "Really? Can you describe them? Maybe they know Philip."

"I didn't look at them too closely."

I had to bite my tongue to keep from asking if one had red hair and the other blond. "What'd they say?"

"One of 'em said Philip traveled all the way here to see Mr. Jacobsen, and the old dude went out of town."

My heart accelerated. Had Angel given us a lead?

She smiled big. "I'm so glad you're going out with him."

"Thanks."

My head swirled with thoughts of thieves as Missy entered with a spring in her step. "Good morning."

A striking woman with hazel eyes and olive skin, Missy ran five miles three times a week and sported a school-girl figure. She'd married Kirby Longman, one of the wealthiest men in Triville. Most recently she spent her time working for charities here and in Misty Gorge.

"Hi, what are we doing today?" I wandered over to the shampoo bowl, and she sat down in the chair.

"If you have time, I'd like an up-do."

"Sure. Do you want to choose from the hairstylist magazine?"

"Just a French twist."

Whew. I'd wind that up quickly. I leaned her back and performed my ritual. Then she walked to the first styling station.

"How's little Ryan? I bet he's grown since the last time I saw him." I combed through her locks.

"Yes, he's walking now."

I picked up the hair blower.

"I nearly lost him in the drugstore."

The drugstore. I perked up. Had she seen the men? I couldn't remember when there'd been so much talk of strangers in town out of tourist season.

"Scared me to death when I looked down and he was gone. I finally found him in the back of the store playing with a stuffed sheep. Kids must have an invisible antenna that leads them to toys."

"Thank goodness, you found him."

"I'd been concentrating so hard on the wrinkle removers I didn't see where he went. I was asking myself if I wanted a moisturizer with or without an SPF. Then I noticed one with skin toner and yet another with an anti-gravity agent." Missy giggled. "I wasn't sure if I was more dry, wrinkled, or saggy."

I laughed. "You're much too young for wrinkled or saggy, and you look fantastic. I heard someone in there was talking about Philip Wells and Mr. Jacobsen. Did you catch that conversation?"

"I completely forgot. You've been dating Philip, haven't you?"

"Yes." I put down the hair blower and brushed the tangles out of Missy's hair.

"Now that you mention it, two men discussed them. One of them said Mr. Jacobsen lives on top of a mountain. Who doesn't know that? He asked the other where Philip was staying, and the guy said Philip was at the Triville Motel. Is that right?"

I held in a gasp. "Yes. When were you in the drugstore?"

Missy touched her forefinger to her lips. "A couple weeks ago."

My breath quickened, and I sucked in air as I started winding Missy's hair in the twist. "What did they look like?"

Missy bit her bottom lip. "I don't recall. Actually, I don't think I saw them face to face. I remember catching Philip's name in a conversation as I looked for

Ryan. It registered with me because I know he's here to see Corley, and that you've been dating him."

Heat pricked my cheeks. Did no one realize Philip would soon be gone, and I'd be left here alone? Even if they didn't, the important thing now was to find that money. "Did you hear them say anything else, or did they mention where they were staying?"

"No, why?" Missy's voice sounded confused.

"I just wondered if they're someone Philip met at the motel, or if they're here from New York."

"Oh. Sorry, I don't know." Missy seemed satisfied with my explanation.

Two people may have seen the thieves, and I'd gotten so little information from them. A silent scream echoed in my head as I sprayed Missy's hair. A sweet-smelling mist fell around us as I gave her the hand mirror and swiveled her chair. Could Philip hang out at the drugstore, put the place under his surveillance, and follow the criminals from there?

Missy smiled while gazing at the up-do. "I have to make a speech in Misty Gorge this evening. This is perfect." She stood, smoothed the wrinkles out of her brown skirt, gave me her payment, and left.

I grabbed the broom and swept to calm my nerves and ease the irritation that nagged me for not being able to learn more.

The door opened.

"Come in." I darted to the back, put away the broom, and hurried up front.

Janie Wannmaker carried a green, soft-shell cooler, her long, auburn hair a mess with split ends. "How's it goin'?"

"I'm having a great day."

Janie often needed to rush back to the office to

assist her husband, Donnie, our mayor. When she was young she loved helping her mother in her flower shop, but she'd given up her passion to work as Donnie's secretary.

"When you finish my permanent, it'll be lunchtime. I thought we could have a bite to eat before you style my hair." She held up the container.

"How kind of you. I'll deduct it from your price."

"Absolutely not. I can't remember all the times you've given me a soft drink." Janie glanced toward the back of the shop. "I thought I'd bum one off you today."

"Sure. I'll grab it while your permanent sets." In no time I zipped through washing, conditioning, and rinsing.

She stood, went to the hairstyling station, and took the chair closest to the back.

I finished parting off the sections, rolling up the curlers, and squirting each with solution by eleven o'clock. "I'll be right back with your drink." I patted her shoulder then dashed to the supply closet, snatched a beverage from the bottom shelf, and returned.

Philip stood in the middle of the room.

I nearly dropped Janie's drink. What was he doing here?

"Could I get a haircut?"

I pulled the soda tight against my chest, glanced at the clock, and then back at Janie.

Her eyes lit up as she held out her hand. "I'll take that. You tend to him."

He peered at me with his sad puppy look.

"All right." I motioned toward her. "This is Janie Wannmaker."

They exchanged greetings then Philip situated himself in the shampoo bowl seat and leaned back. I wet his hair and added the creamy liquid. The warmth from his head triggered my memory of us in the river at the Western Hills Festival, and I wished he would hold me again. I rubbed circles around his temples.

"I got nothing at the diner this morning. Have you heard anything?" he whispered.

His voice brought me to the moment. I wanted to talk to him about the drugstore, but I couldn't in front of Janie. My hands flew around his head as I scrubbed. "Not really, but I have one thing to mention."

He sat up while I towel-dried his hair. Then he stepped to the salon chair, plopped down and met my gaze in the mirror, his brow furrowed. "Somebody in this town knows what's going on. This is day two. What did you find out? I'll go back to the diner and stay until those thieves show. Then I'll follow them. They'll be sorry they stole anything from me." Philip's entire body tensed.

He might do something foolish and get hurt as keyed up as he was, or worse yet…my heart beat like a jackhammer. "No. Wait. We'll do this together."

Janie glanced toward us.

"Yes. I think everybody loves the daisies in the park this year." This was the last place to discuss anything private.

He jerked his head, and I nearly nicked his neck. "Sit still."

"Sorry. Why are you talking about flowers?"

I leaned over and flipped his bangs. "How short do you want these?" I pinched him on the shoulder and whispered, "Later."

"Ouch. Fine. Uh, just trim them if you don't

mind."

Philip's distraught look wrenched my heart. Even if I couldn't see him after he left, I vowed to find those thieves. I finished his haircut, and he stood and pulled his billfold out of his back pants pocket.

"Oh, you. Treat me tonight at dinner."

"It's a deal. What time?"

"Eight o'clock. I'm working late."

"See ya' then."

Philip strode outside as Janie's buzzer sounded.

She stood and charged to the shampoo bowl. "I'm glad that part's done. I always hate the smell."

"Ah, but it's worth it. You'll look gorgeous."

I applied the neutralizer, rinsed her hair, and patted it dry.

She rubbed her stomach. "Now for the fun part. I'm starving. Can you style and blow my hair after lunch?"

"Sure. Let's eat in the kitchen." I had to block Philip's problem from my mind and tend to my customer. Any other day I'd have nothing else to do and would welcome the company, especially one who brought lunch.

But now I worried about Philip. He'd be all right if he returned to the diner. But what if he saw the red head and the blond and trailed them on his own?

A shiver ran up my spine as Janie and I left the shop. We crossed the pebble driveway and grassy patch of yard to the porch. I opened the front door and tried not to worry about Philip.

"It'd be nice if Donnie had given me the day off, but I have to answer all the emails before I leave tonight. You'd think I was the mayor." Janie chuckled as we followed the hallway to the kitchen.

The coffee pot sat in the sink, my empty cup where I'd left it on the counter this morning. I snatched it up, wiped off the table, and swung open the fridge door. "Let me see, I'll contribute strawberries."

Janie pulled a straight chair out from the table and plopped down as I set a couple plates. Then I joined her and poured a fizzing soda into her glass as she opened the cooler and handed me a sandwich.

"Pimento cheese, one of my favorites."

She swallowed. "Uh-huh, mine too. Tell me about Philip."

"There's not much to say. He's passing through town." My heart flip-flopped hoping he was safe and sound.

"Yeah, I heard he landed a large brokerage account with Corley Jacobsen. The way that old dude stays to himself, I'm amazed he'd do business with anyone. Philip must be quite a guy." Janie picked up a strawberry and popped it in her mouth.

Yes, he was, but I could barely focus on Janie's hairdo for agonizing about Philip's situation, let alone discuss him. "He is."

"Mr. Jacobsen doesn't trust banks. No telling where he keeps his money. It could be buried in the backyard."

A soft snort escaped my nose as I nearly choked on my soft drink.

"Everyone's gossiping about them, but Mr. Jacobsen's so tight-lipped. No one knows Philip well enough to comment on his affairs." Janie wiped her mouth. "They don't know what they're talking about. Of course, I'm not sure they ever do." She laughed.

Why must Janie talk about Philip and the money? My nerves shifted into high gear for fear he would stop at nothing to recoup the million dollars. I forced a weak chuckle at Janie's joke. Had she heard something that would lead Philip and me to the thieves? "I don't have anything to add, but I'm interested in hearing the latest." I nibbled on the last of my sandwich and swallowed.

"Nothing concrete. Everyone's speculating on how much money Corley will invest and whether or not he'll give Philip cash."

I couldn't breathe. Wondering and actually knowing something were two different things. So far everything she'd said was mere conjecture.

Janie sipped her drink. "Some are asking how long Philip will stay here." Janie tilted her head. "I figured you'd know that."

I nearly jumped out of my skin for wanting to get back to the shop and drop this subject. "Not really." I picked up our trash and tossed it in the garbage can.

Janie flashed me a sheepish grin as she brought the dishes to the sink. "It's not every evening couples go to Frank's General Store to weigh after hours."

I buried my head in my hands and shook it, but it didn't make the embarrassment go away. I looked up. "That entire incident was a big misunderstanding."

"Uh-huh." Janie patted me on the shoulder. "I'm just teasing." She sat down and peered at me with a distant look in her eyes. "I still remember the day you and Jordan married. I can see him smiling as though he'd won the lottery standing at the altar waiting for you."

My knees nearly buckled.

"I think Jordan fell in love with you in grammar school. You were blessed to have someone who adored you."

"I was crazy about him too. He was my whole life." I fought back tears.

"I understand. What happened to him was so tragic, but do you know what he'd want more than anything?"

How could she possibly know what Jordan would want? "I have an idea you'll tell me."

"He's watching from above and he'd much rather see you enjoying yourself than looking sad."

She was right. She made it sound so simple.

"Give Philip a chance. He seems like a great guy."

The necklace Jordan gave me hung heavy around my neck. I fingered it. "I do think a lot of Philip, but after his business with Mr. Jacobsen, I may never see him again."

"People's plans change. Even if Philip is just passing through town, when he leaves maybe he'll take you with him."

"That's what Ellie said. I've never lived anywhere but Triville. I don't think I could leave."

Janie stiffened her jaw. "You could if it meant you would be with someone who loved you, and you loved him. Don't shut any doors."

Aggravation tingled on my skin. She seemed to see mine and Philip's complicated situation so clearly. In my heart I knew she meant well. She only wanted me to be happy. "I won't. Let's wrap up your new hairdo." I switched off the kitchen light and made tracks down the hall, out the door, and over to Eve's Clips, Janie with me step for step.

I finished her style, and she left. What she said about Jordan wanting me to be happy made sense. For the life of me, I didn't know why I'd never thought of that. Maybe it was because Jordan was in Heaven, and

I was here, and that nearly drove me crazy. She had a point though.

The rest of the day I washed, blow-dried, snipped, and curled, thinking of Philip all the while. My last customer left at seven-fifteen.

I couldn't wait to get my shower and see Philip. Whatever our relationship was now, might or might not be in the future, I needed to know he was safe.

18

I wrapped my housecoat around me as the light streaming in the bedroom window waned and the sun set. Philip would arrive soon. I turned on the lamp on the wicker nightstand, and the click echoed in the room. Sure enough, the doorbell rang as I pulled on a pair of gray pants. I threw on a royal blue blouse and answered.

"Hi, I'm itching to know what you found out in the shop. I've never seen Bob's as dead as it was today. Of course, when I wanted those creeps to come in, no one ate lunch there but a couple state troopers, several groups of women, and two ladies with babies."

Thank goodness. He could've gotten himself in a dangerous situation if those hoodlums had shown. "That is unusual." I put my arms around his neck and hugged him. "I don't know if it's important or not, but Angel Epps and Missy Longman overheard two strangers in the drugstore mention you and Mr. Jacobsen. Missy said they discussed where you were staying. Remember, we wondered if someone cased out your room. It's possible they did."

Philip's eyes widened. "Mr. Jacobsen's so eccentric. I bet somebody figured out he'd hand me the cash, but who? I'd like to eat in Merchantville where we can talk without anyone in Triville hearing us."

"OK."

He helped me into the old car, drove through

town, and headed toward the expressway. "This thing's amazing. She keeps humming along."

"Lloyd's a talent."

Philip leaned back in his seat as though he enjoyed driving to the Airport Central Hotel. He parked then helped me out of the car and put his arm around my waist as we followed a sidewalk illuminated with in-ground lights. We whirled in a revolving door that opened to a huge lobby filled with people winding around plush leather chairs and potted plants.

Philip marched to an open-air cafe with a brass rail in the back of the room and approached the host. "Could we sit there, please?" He pointed to a waterfall running over a rocky wall from the second story into a small pool lined with ferns and large dieffenbachia plants.

"Sure." The host escorted us to a black wrought iron table beside the cascade and laid down two menus. "Enjoy your meal."

Philip scooted his chair as close to the water as he could. "Move over."

I did.

He pulled up the table. "This is perfect. The roar will obscure everything we say." He patted the back of my seat.

"If we don't drown and we can hear each other."

Philip laughed.

It was good to see his mood lighten.

"What would you like to drink?" The waiter seemed to appear out of nowhere.

Philip placed his palm on the menu. "Do you have sweet tea in Merchantville?"

"Yes, sir."

"I'll have that with the roasted turkey, mashed

potatoes, and cranberry jelly."

"That sounds good. The same for me, please."

The waiter left and Philip peered at me with anxious blue eyes. "OK, what did these guys in the drugstore look like? Do you think they were the same two we saw at Bob's Diner?"

"I suspect they are. Unfortunately, neither Angel nor Missy could describe them."

Philip stiffened. "How's that possible?"

"They were both pre-occupied with something else. Of course, Mandy probably could detail everyone who entered the store, but if we asked her, she'd not only insist on knowing why we inquired, she'd tell everyone who came in we were interested in two strangers. They'd all speculate on..."

Philip held up his hand before I finished the sentence. "No. We don't want to involve Mandy."

The waiter served our food then Philip leaned closer to me. "Does anyone in town know Mr. Jacobsen keeps money in the freezer?" he whispered.

I sipped my drink. Apparently, he intended to take no chances, even though we were miles from the inquiring ears of Triville. "He's so reclusive. I don't think so."

Philip cut off a bite of turkey.

If he hadn't taken time to deal with my supplies he might have made more progress solving his problem and he wouldn't be so stressed. I had to help him, but I didn't know what to do. "Why don't we enjoy our dinner and then brainstorm. I've never been in this hotel. It's beautiful."

"We'll have to come back often."

He wouldn't be close enough to return to this hotel. If he lived up to his claim to fly in on the weekends, I could meet him here on Thursday or Friday evenings. Now I was starting to think like him. It was all a big fantasy, but I didn't want to say anything to upset him anymore than he already was.

We scraped our plates, and the waiter showed up to take our dessert orders.

I asked for tiramisu, and Philip did too.

He looked as though he'd run a marathon and was about to collapse from exhaustion.

I rubbed my temples as if the action would activate my brain cells, and I'd find an answer. It didn't, but the repetitive motion made me block out everything around me and concentrate. "It has to be the strangers who took Mr. Jacobsen's money. No one I know personally would steal. I'm friends with nearly everybody in Triville, or I was before I ruined their hair."

"Now that you have decent products they'll look like movie stars."

"Movie stars?" I chuckled.

The waiter served our treats.

"Do you think these dudes will come back to the drugstore? Should I hang out there?" Philip scooped up a forkful of dessert.

I'd wondered the same thing. "It'd be a start."

The waiter placed the bill on the table.

Philip paid then we left and trekked to the car.

"I'll be in that drugstore tomorrow if and when these guys return. They'll not slip by me." Determination lined Philip's voice as he backed out.

"If you see them and they leave, follow them at a safe distance. Don't confront them or do anything dangerous until we have time to come up with a plan, and I can go with you."

Philip grunted.

I took it as an agreement.

Philip pulled onto the interstate toward Triville and took off. In no time it seemed he'd gotten off the expressway, turned into my driveway, and parked. "If the thieves are professionals they could copy a motel key card. What if I didn't put the bolt on the door?"

"Oh, no. That could explain the theft." I thought for a moment. "It's too late to change that now, but I think you're onto something. See what you can do tomorrow in the drugstore, and I'll keep my ears open in the shop." With every bone in my body I wanted to encourage Philip and then nail those criminals.

He accompanied me to the door, ran his hand from my cheek to my neck and pulled me close. His lips brushed against mine then he kissed me deep and long.

"I'm exhausted. I have to get some rest, so I'll be alert tomorrow." He peered at me with steady eyes. "My future...our future depends on getting back the money soon."

How could we have a future?

I grabbed him around the neck and hugged him tight. "Good luck with your sleuthing."

"Thanks, I'll call. We'll get together tomorrow night."

"We won't give up until you have the cash back."

Philip plodded to the car with his head lowered.

What did Philip mean by our future? His words played in my head. But first, we had to recover Mr. Jacobsen's investment.

19

Philip drove back to the motel past closed shops and offices illuminated with lamppost lighting. He paid little attention to the hum of the motor cutting into the quiet night. How could he have been so careless? From the instant Mr. Jacobsen handed him those duffle bags he thought only of getting the money to a bank in New York. He never imagined he needed to be careful leaving Triville. The whole look of the town, the way it nestled into the mountains. The neat streets and pristine yards screamed of innocence. Now he knew. There was no such place.

He parked in front of his room, darted inside, and made a beeline to the shower. His muscles ached from the events of the day. Hoping for rest, he hopped out, put on his pajamas as fast as he could, and fell into bed.

"Strangers," Eve had said. Tomorrow he'd find those out-of-towners, follow them like a hound, and spy on them. Then he'd retrieve that money. If he slept well he'd be alert for the task.

He tossed and turned, threw back the covers, and sat on the edge of the bed. The outside light streamed through a crack where the thick-backed curtains failed to meet and shone on a newspaper in front of his door. Someone must have delivered it while he was in the bathroom. He got up, brought it to the bed, and switched on the lamp. Reading it, his eyelids grew heavy and he fell asleep.

~*~

A buzz pierced Philip's ears. Sitting straight up, he grabbed the alarm clock. He'd intended to set it for seven and arrive at the drugstore at seven-thirty. It was eight now.

He bounded off the bed, brushed his teeth, and tugged on a pair of jeans. Standing beside the cubbyhole closet, he snatched a blue shirt, threw it on, and buttoned it on the way outside. He drove to the drugstore entrance as fast as the old car would take him and parked.

Inside the store, a country music song played softly from hidden speakers.

Mandy stood. "Good morning can I help you?"

"No, thank you." Philip dashed past the bottles, boxes, and rolled-up blankets lining the shelves near the front.

"What are you looking for?"

If he entered a drugstore in New York someone might say hello. After that, they'd mind their own business. He had intended to wander around the premises all day. The townspeople's penchant for knowing everything about everyone had slipped his mind. He glanced back at Mandy. "Razors. I need razors."

"They're on aisle seven." Mandy plopped down on her stool.

Philip wandered to the section for men's toiletries, picked up a package of shavers, and carried them to check-out.

Mandy rang up his purchase. "I see you found them." A cheerful lilt filled her voice.

"Yes."

She stuffed the items into a bag and handed it to him. "Thanks for shopping at Smitty's."

His left eye twitched as he trudged out and plopped down in the car. He couldn't leave now.

A vehicle pulled up beside him, and his heartbeat accelerated. *Strangers?* He glanced out the window. Two women emerged from a red sedan and chattered to each other as they hurried to the entrance. A young couple pushed a stroller behind them, and an old man bumped along on a walker. Philip sprang out and opened the door for the elderly gentleman then returned to his stakeout.

A boring parade of shoppers passed until a man in a lightweight brown jacket appeared at noon, a hat over his head and his collar turned up covering part of his face. Philip eased out of the car and passed through the doorway on the man's heels.

"Hello, Graham." Mandy stood and smiled.

The man tipped his hat.

He clearly wasn't one of the strangers. *Back to the car.*

"Why hello, again." Mandy's cheerful voice rang out.

Too late. "Hi." Philip had to think fast. "How's it goin'? I need a bite of lunch."

Mandy waved her small hand toward the soda fountain. "We serve great grilled cheese sandwiches."

Philip proceeded to the eatery and found a booth facing the entrance. This site made a better stake-out than the car. Mandy's reaction to whoever came inside would indicate whether or not that person lived in

Triville. He was getting the hang of small town America.

The waitress came over. "Hi, I'm Teresa. What can I get for you?"

"Ah, could I start with a glass of sweet tea?"

"Sure, hon. Whatever you want." She left and returned quickly with his drink. "What else would you like?"

"If you don't mind, check back in a little while." Philip grabbed a menu from behind a vase of artificial roses and pretended to study it. This set-up put him right in the middle of the action, and finally he was inconspicuous. He glanced at the seven entrees on the bill of fare then focused on the front door.

Mandy greeted patron after patron. Philip's confidence in his stakeout fell, but he persisted. He turned up his glass—empty.

Teresa hurried over with the tea pitcher. "Here ya' go, sir. Are you ready to order?"

"Yes please, I'll have a grilled cheese sandwich, French fries, and a side salad with ranch dressing."

Teresa wrote on her pad.

She has no idea what I'm up to. Finally, he'd hidden something from someone in Triville. His pride in his snooping ability heightened. He'd watched the entrance like a trained professional. Nothing had escaped him and nothing would.

"I believe you 'bout waited too long to order. Sounds like you worked up an appetite sitting in the booth."

"I can eat."

"Comin' right up." She called out his request to thin air, but someone had to be in the kitchen.

Teresa returned and set down his food. "There ya'

go. Hope ya' enjoy it."

Philip's mouth watered, but he couldn't gulp down the meal. He had to bide his time and not miss a single person coming in the doorway. Having the hours tick away without seeing the strangers set his nerves on edge. One by one the diners at the soda fountain and in the booths left. Only he remained, his hard detective work unrewarded. He slumped in his seat.

Teresa appeared and filled his glass as a man with blond hair entered. He straightened. "Who's that?"

Teresa shifted her gaze. "Jerry Wilburn. He's probably here to get his wife's arthritis medicine. It's a shame. She's housebound now." Compassion filled her hazel eyes.

Philip's optimism deflated. He felt sorry for a woman he'd never seen. Had the caring attitude of Triville's residents rubbed off on him? "That's sad."

"Yeah, it is. Do ya' want dessert?"

"Yes, please. I'll have an apple cobbler with vanilla ice cream and coffee."

"Sure thing." Teresa left and returned with the sweet treat. "Are ya' just a slow eater, or ain't ya' got nothin' to do?"

"I'm sorry. Am I keeping you late?"

"Not really. There's nothin' waitin' for me but one no account husband and his no account hound dog."

"Come on, now. Did you grow up here?"

"Yep. I'm teasin.' I graduated from Triville High School and married Ray Bounts, a football star. We won all our games when he was the quarterback."

"Sounds like a great guy."

Teresa grinned. "He is. He woulda' gone to college on a scholarship, but he got hurt his senior year."

"I'm sorry."

"It's OK. Everyone still calls him Bullet Bounts. He loves it. He's a sweet man, and we're happy. Life ain't worth livin' if you ain't happy, and you won't be happy unless you love the spirit."

"You're a smart woman enjoying success others only dream about." That seemed to be the case with most of the folks in Triville. He yearned to enjoy the peace he'd found here permanently and acquire the same quiet acceptance of others they seemed to have. If only he could get back the money, he could make plans.

A wide grin spread across Teresa's face as she laid down a bill. "I'll leave this, but I'm here until four o'clock if you need anything else."

Philip ate his cobbler and placed his payment, plus a generous tip for Teresa, on the table.

Two strangers stood at the counter handing a pack of cigarettes to Mandy.

Philip rose from his seat, knocked over a plate, and righted it while keeping his gaze on them as they exited. He made tracks toward the door and held his hand up at the register. "I don't need a thing. Stay put."

Mandy waved. "Have a great day."

He breezed through the doorway, darted into the car, and frantically looked for the pickup. A white blur passed by him. He pulled out and ended up behind a tour bus in a no-passing zone unable to see anything except the rear of the large vehicle. His heart beat like a jackhammer until he could pass. He accelerated and zoomed up the road. There were no white trucks in sight. The men were just here. Where did they go? How could they have gotten away so quickly?

His stomach knotted as he drove to the motel. He parked, entered his unit, and put on the bolt. Either Triville wasn't the sleepy little town it seemed or somebody up to no good infiltrated this mountain paradise. He checked e-mail, praying his boss hadn't discovered the theft yet. Nothing was out of the ordinary. Philip breathed a sigh of relief.

Eve may have heard something about strangers in town from one of her customers. He splashed on fresh cologne and headed over there. Hope for answers pulsed through his veins all the way to Eve's Clips. He entered with anticipation filling him. "Hi." He waited patiently as she turned from blow-drying a lady's blonde hair.

"Hello. I have a message for you. Lloyd's repaired the rent-a-car, but he's gone out of town, so you can pick it up Monday."

"Is that all?" Her words dampened his spirits, but she might tell him more later. "OK, thanks. How about dinner?"

"Sure, Philip. I'd like that."

He sat down underneath a hair dryer and tapped his foot while Eve finished her customer's hair. If only the two of them could find these guys.

The client left and Eve asked, "Any leads?"

"Yes, I saw them, but they escaped." Heat crawled up his neck.

"We're getting close. I'll go change really quick."

Before Philip knew it, Eve reappeared looking stunning in a black and white dress, He guided her to the old car, and they breezed over the level streets in town.

"Did you find out anything in the shop?" He thumped his fingers on the steering wheel.

"I'm sorry. Not today, but we're on the right track. We'll probably see those strangers or hear something about them tonight. Obviously, they're hanging out in Triville."

His time was running out. "Yeah. I thought one of your customers would know who they are and mention them."

Eve patted his arm. "It will work out."

He started up the hill, the car's stops and starts now commonplace. Finally, he reached the parking lot and cut the engine. They hurried inside, where the smell of chili cheeseburgers wafted in the front of the room. They took the first booth, and Eve leaned forward. "This is perfect. From here we can check out everybody."

"I have a crick in my neck from my day at the drugstore, but I'm an expert at scrutinizing people entering establishments."

"Take a break. I have the entrance covered."

Bonnie Sue sashayed over. "How's it goin'? I haven't seen you since pot roast night." She winked at Philip then popped her gum.

"We're fine." Philip made a point of saying "we," and hoped Eve caught it. There was no one for him but Eve.

Bonnie Sue gave him her flirty grin. "What ya' going to have?"

"A chili cheeseburger."

"Eve?" Bonnie Sue glanced at her.

"I'll take the same."

Bonnie Sue left, and Eve stood. "I'll wander to the bathroom and see who else is here." She headed toward the back, disappeared into the crowd then returned and scooted in the booth. "No strangers yet," she whispered.

Bonnie Sue set down two steaming plates. "Enjoy," she said. Then she waved at the Saturday night patrons jamming in. "Hi ya'll. It won't be long till some seats come open."

Eve touched Philip's leg with her foot under the table and nodded her head toward the door.

He pivoted slightly then glanced at two men approaching the take out counter. His heartbeat pounded in his temples. He wiped his mouth, casually laid down his napkin, and then sprang from his seat. Eve stood as he snatched up the bill and followed as he forged to the cash register. The instant the cashier handed him change, he guided Eve out the door, past the people in the parking lot, and into the passenger's side of the old car.

He slipped into the driver's seat as Eve fidgeted with her purse.

"Don't we look odd sitting outside in the car?" she asked.

"We wouldn't be noticed in New York, but here, you could be right."

Philip sprang out and raised the hood, all the while keeping his gaze on the door to the diner.

Footsteps fell behind him.

He jumped.

"What's wrong, son? Having trouble? I know a little about cars. Want me to take a look?" Reverend Binder asked.

Philip's nerves raced. He had to drive out of here the instant he saw those strangers. He should've known in Triville someone would stop to help.

"Thanks, I think we're OK." Philip jiggled the first wire he saw under the hood.

Reverend Binder patted Philip on the back. "Hop in there and see if it starts."

Philip tried to look around the minister to the door, but couldn't get a clear view. Heaviness fell on his chest. What if the strangers · had exited the restaurant? "Thanks." He plopped down in the driver's seat, left the door open, and kept his gaze on the entrance to Bob's Diner as best he could. His hand trembled as he turned the key. The car hummed.

Reverend Binder gave him a thumbs' up. "Call my cell phone if you have any trouble. Eve knows the number. You kids have fun." He moseyed off.

Philip stared at the diner. The two out-of-towners traipsed out the door and nearly knocked down Reverend Binder as he started inside. The hair on Philip's arms stood on end as he waited for the thieves to reach their vehicle and leave.

20

Soft spotlights lighting up the parking lot at Bob's Diner lent a tranquil glow to the trees and foliage next to the white truck. The strangers climbed into it and pulled out of their parking space as a parade of vehicles drove through the entrance. An old sedan, a van, and an SUV blocked Philip's view of the thieves. He clenched the steering wheel and gritted his teeth. He couldn't lose them again. Finally, the incoming traffic settled, and he backed out. "Watch for the pick-up."

Eve leaned forward and swiped her forehead as Philip turned right.

"I believe it's in front of the black SUV. Thank goodness, we're going downhill. Maybe we can pass."

The SUV turned onto a side road.

Philip's muscles tensed with a sense of urgency as he closed in on the suspects' vehicle. At last his headlights hit the back of the truck and he took a sigh of relief. "Write down the license number."

Eve pulled a pen and piece of paper out of her purse and moved to the edge of her seat. "Got it. Back off."

Philip slowed down and cruised behind the truck until the strangers turned onto the expressway leading to Merchantville. Cars, vans, and SUVs whizzed by as the vehicle darted in and out of lanes.

Eve sat straight up. "Get closer. We're losing

them."

The truck whipped onto a ramp.

Following, Philip glanced at the directional sign. "Have you ever been to Chapsburg?"

"Oddly, I haven't." Eve sat back in her seat. "When I was in high school, it was in an area known as a hotbed of crime. Can you imagine that around here?"

"After having the money stolen, sure, I imagine there are major league criminals in these hills."

"I haven't thought about the place in years, but it's all coming together. I knew it would." Eve snapped her fingers. "Years ago we heard the gangsters they caught were convicted of car theft, making counterfeit money, and gambling."

Philip could smell Mr. Jacobsen's cash. "Looks like the feds left a little dirt behind."

"Big-time mobsters, I think." Eve's voice sounded shaky, but Philip's dogged purpose drove him onward.

"I don't want to put you in danger, but I have to tail this vehicle. I can do it, and they'll never know." He followed the truck onto a dirt road.

Eve gasped. "There's no telling where we're headed now."

Philip rode farther into the dark passageway, and his stomach knotted at the danger of getting trapped in this isolated area. He cut his headlights. "I understand. I'll creep along and stay back."

The pick-up's taillights moved to the left.

Philip zipped in behind the vehicle, and beams of light illuminated a long driveway from the corners of an old, wooden house. "It looks as though they pulled into a residence, clicked on the lights from a remote, and got out."

"Uh-huh." Eve mumbled softly.

Thank goodness, the men were facing away from the car as they motored toward the home. With a shaky hand, Philip shoved the gear shift into reverse. *Please don't make racket. Don't stall.* He backed into the shadows in tall grass on the shoulder of the road.

The guys meandered onto the front porch, put something in a wooden box, and went inside.

He'd found the thieves. Thankfulness seeped into Philip's pores as he got out and closed the car door. "I'll be right back. I'll take a closer look."

Eve bounded out. "You're not leaving me." Terror filled her eyes.

He'd never forgive himself if anything happened to her. "Now I know where they live. I'll come back later."

"It's OK. I'm fine. I don't want you out there alone. I was a little nervous at first, but you're so smart. I trust you. If we're quiet and careful, we can do this."

The way those hoodlums disappeared inside without even a glance around the yard, they didn't suspect a thing.

"Follow me." Philip pointed to a row of pines and hardwoods. "Let's duck behind those trees where the lights aren't as bright."

"OK."

"When we get close to the house, we can't talk. If you're afraid and need to leave, or if something looks dangerous to you, tap my arm three times." Philip demonstrated. "I'll do the same."

Eve's breath sounded ragged as she whispered, "All right."

They squatted behind a huge towering oak.

Philip crept from one tree to another with Eve on his heels. He didn't stop advancing until they were parallel with the rear of the house.

The two men stood on the back porch. Bright spotlights shone on their lips as they spoke, but Philip couldn't make out the words. They wandered into the yard and tramped no more than five feet from Philip and Eve. Philip's heart thumped so hard he worried they'd heard it.

"We've staked out the car lot. It's time to make our plan and do it." The man wearing the blue-checked shirt tapped the red-headed guy on the arm.

Red Head stopped in his tracks. "Let's go over their inventory one more time."

"Why? We saw the ones we want to strip." Blue-checked Shirt paced back and forth through the tall grass.

Red Head shrugged his shoulders. "Ta' make sure they didn't get in anything new."

The two men meandered away from Eve and Philip toward a narrow, steep canyon with a swinging bridge. They stomped onto it, and the planks and ropes swayed with every step they took. Yet, they crossed it, and disappeared.

Philip tapped Eve three times. "Come on."

"Come on? I thought you were alerting me to danger." She knitted her eyebrows. "You said we couldn't talk."

"I know, but they can't hear us now. We need to follow them."

Eve stood and brushed off her jeans. "Believe me, when you start across that flimsy, homemade contraption, you'll wish you'd never set foot on it. Look, it's still swinging from the two guys walking over it."

"It's intimidating, but I have to find the money."

Mr. Jacobsen's cash and the future Philip wanted for Eve and him pulled him toward the scant framework.

"Where will we hide if they start back across?"

She had him there.

"Can we drop down and hold onto the planks?"

"Yeah, and get our fingers smashed when they stomp on them. You don't want to fall. The canyons around here are rocky and at least one hundred feet straight down." Authority lined Eve's voice.

Philip's insides churned for wanting to trace the thieves' footsteps and find the cash.

"Whoo-whoo."

An owl perched on a tree limb in the glow of the moonlight. This was a forest filled with God's creatures, and they were at peace. "We'll wait here. When they come back and enter the house, we'll go across."

The muscles in Eve's face relaxed. "Yes. We could do that."

Philip gave her a hug. "God will protect us."

"Then nothing can stop us."

They squatted down behind the trees. The owl's whoo, whoo cut into the quiet night again, and this could have been any backyard. The tall grass moved as a brown rabbit hopped toward Eve and Philip. Three feet from them, it sat up straight and wiggled its nose. Philip glanced at Eve. "Does it know we're here?"

"Uh-huh. Probably. Us, the possums, and raccoons."

"My legs are tired." Philip dropped down on the ground. "I hope I'm not sitting on ants."

"I'd worry more about snakes. I wish those creeps would come back, so we could get this over with." Eve joined him.

Philip put his finger over his lips. "Shhh. I hear something."

Checked-Blue Shirt and Red Head trudged across the backyard and went inside. The spotlights blinked off, but the glow from the porch bulb still shone. It along with the moon and twinkling stars lent enough light to see.

Philip stood and sticks broke underneath him. "That bridge held both of those guys. The red-haired fellow weighs at least two hundred pounds, and the other one about that much. It'll support the two of us."

Eve rose and they crept toward the rickety structure, staying in the shadow of the house.

Philip halted. Seeing the apparatus up close made his blood run cold. "Don't worry. We'll be fine." Philip meant to reassure Eve, but he said the words with more hope than certainty. "I'll go first." If the whole thing collapsed, maybe it'd do it before Eve set foot on it. He sucked in air and tapped a plank with one foot. The entire frame shook. His nerves cracked as he placed both feet on the wobbly pedestrian walkway and grabbed a rope. The wooden crossing rocked, and his head spun, but Eve's hot breath fell on the back of his neck. Courage raced up his spine.

A spotlight brightened the backyard.

Philip's heart pounded. "Swing below."

"I'm not…"

"Hurry. I won't let you drop." He spoke softly when he wanted to scream as he grasped two slats, lowered his body, and hung in mid-air above the rocky canyon.

Eve eased down and clasped two boards as another spotlight illuminated the entire yard and bridge. Her left hand slipped off. Horror radiated from her eyes.

Philip reached out and pushed her toward the structure. "You're fine." His calm tone disguised the panic surging through him.

The planks wiggled, and Eve's free hand flew back.

Philip's pulse throbbed in his temples as fear gripped him. He let go with his right hand and propelled her forward. "Grab hold."

Her fingertips swiped a board.

"Take it."

Her arm swung backward.

Philip's brain froze. A force inside him moved his body as though he wasn't in it. He bumped into Eve and thrust her toward the lumber. "Reach out. Clench it. Do it."

Her head slung forward. Her torso followed. Her fingers touched the wood, and she clutched it.

How long could she hold on? If anything happened to her, the money didn't matter.

The two men headed toward them. "Where do you think you left it?"

Philip recognized the red-haired man's voice.

"It's in the warehouse. You hurried me," the man in the blue-checked shirt said.

"Yeah, yeah, every time you do something stupid, it's my fault. I have on my pajamas already." Red Head's voice sounded angry.

"You don't have to come. I'll go alone." The structure moved as Blue-Checked Shirt stepped on it.

Philip squelched a gasp and prayed for God to hold up Eve and him.

"Na, I'm comin.' Or we could wait 'til tomorrow. There ain't nothin' out here to shoot but rabbits and possums."

Philip stopped breathing. What was he thinking getting this close to two criminals and bringing someone who meant so much to him? He'd acted on the spur of the moment because he believed finding the money was the most important thing in his life. Only after he landed Mr. Jacobsen's account could he pursue the dreams he had for Eve and him, and live with the peace he'd found in Triville. He'd let his vision cloud his mind, but he could see clearly now.

"I guess I ain't goin' to need the gun while I'm sleepin'."

"Oy, that's the phone ringing. Get back in the house. We'll get it tomorrow."

Philip exhaled.

Leaves rustled and then the spotlights went out.

"Eve, are you all right? Can you climb up?" She looked like a statue with eyes popped as far open as they would go. Guilt gushed through Philip. He gave her as much of a boost as he could, and she pushed her upper body onto the rocking bridge. He hoisted himself up, pulled her close, and held her tight while she shivered. "I almost lost you. It scared me so bad. We'll leave as soon as we rest a minute."

Eve sucked in a deep gulp of air. "They're not coming back out here. We'll find the warehouse then tell Chief Grimes where it is."

Philip brushed her hair from her face. "No. I can't put you in danger again. I couldn't stand it if anything happened to you."

She gave him a light jab on the shoulder. "Nothing will happen. We're doing the right thing, and we've come too far to turn back now. The hard part's behind us. Remember, God's protecting us. Come on."

Eve's words plus the strength and faith radiating from her tone soothed his nerves and convinced him she was right, especially about the worst already occurring. It did appear those goons had gone to bed. "OK, but I have to get the money first. If we tell Chief Grimes, everyone in Triville will know. I can't let that happen." Philip couldn't keep his voice from quivering.

"We'll ask him not to say anything." Eve patted Philip's shoulder.

Philip couldn't help but chuckle. "You mean you, me, and Chief Grimes will have the first secret ever kept in Triville."

Eve snickered. "Come on."

Philip stood. Then he and Eve trod carefully to the other side of the homemade bridge.

He linked arms with her as they proceeded into dense forest. "We're losing the light from their back porch."

"The stars are bright. Our eyes will adjust then we can follow this path."

A ragged boulder stuck out of the ground a few feet ahead.

Philip squeezed Eve's arm. "Get behind me. We'll go around that stone single file." He took one step and fell into a hole up to his waist. He nearly choked, gasping. Where was Eve?

She grabbed his hand and yanked. Thank God she was all right. Starlight and moon-glow shone across her face, tears glistening in her eyes. He planted his feet in the side of the chasm, but the soil beneath him gave way. "I'll find another position then you pull." Philip secured his left foot in the embankment, and once again the earth crumbled. He tumbled back into the pit, and his hand broke loose from Eve's.

Leaves to the right of him moved. A snake slithered out from under them. Terror exploded like fireworks inside Philip, adrenaline rushing through his veins. He placed his hands on the top of the pit and pushed with all his might while he dug the toes of his shoes into the earth and moved his feet as though they were motorized. He slid down, his mind swirling in fright. He grabbed a tree root at the top of the hole and pulled his body upward with strength he didn't know he had. He heaved his legs to the edge of the ditch, rolled out, and stood upright. "OK, I've had enough. Let's leave."

"Look." Eve pointed to the right.

Fifty yards away outdoor lights beamed around a huge concrete block warehouse surrounded with bumpers, car hoods, windshields, and other car parts.

Philip felt a rush of relief. "We made it. We found Mr. Jacobsen's cash." He clutched Eve's hand, and they hurried to the metal side door. He pushed on it with his foot, and it creaked. "I can't believe it's open."

"Why not? No one ever comes out here." Eve followed him through the doorway.

The illumination from outside spotlights shone through a large window exposing a pile of engines and a heap of radios with CD players scattered on the cement floor.

"I'm surprised some hunter hasn't stumbled on this place." Philip shifted a mirror with the toe of his shoe.

"Treacherous terrain few humans have ever trod lies in these hills. I think we're standing on some of it." Eve's eyes widened as she scanned the room.

Philip put his hand on his hip. "How'd they haul

all these car parts up here?"

Eve shook her head. "I don't know. I don't see a way, but maybe they have a make-shift road somewhere out back."

"Could be. It doesn't matter. What matters is finding the money." Philip turned over sheets of scrap metal then picked up radiators one at a time and laid them aside. Nothing. His shoulders slumped as he put everything back so the thieves wouldn't notice anything amiss. He peeked under two old car seats. "Where's the money?" He hadn't intended for the ire to spew into his voice. He ventured to a tiny room that stuck out from the wall. "It's padlocked. It's probably in there." He gazed around. "Do you see the gun Blue-Checked Shirt mentioned?"

"No, and I don't want to. The money is either locked up or not here. We have to tell Chief Grimes about this."

Fear and anger swam deep inside Philip, but of course, he'd never let that surface in front of Eve. He might lose Mr. Jacobsen's account, but what could he do? He stood in this bed of thievery as useless as one of those dead motors. He put his arm around Eve's shoulders, and they trod outdoors. He stopped. No matter what, he must keep Eve safe. "Get behind me and hold onto to my waist."

Eve put both arms around him and marched in his footsteps. They veered to the right to miss the hole and passed by the boulder on the left. Branches and forest underbrush crunched underneath their shoes, but there was no one out here to hear except the wood's creatures. They hiked back onto the path worn smooth with footsteps and reached the bridge. Philip grabbed hold of a rope, keeping the structure as steady as possible for Eve.

She took in a deep breath, planted her foot on the end of a plank and broke into a near run. Philip took off right behind her, the slats rattling, the ropes swinging. He bounded onto the yard and clasped her hand. Then they raced to the car.

The squeak from the old car's door resounded into the quiet night. A light lit up the front porch. Philip rushed to the driver's side and slung himself in, his gut rumbling. He turned the key with a shaking hand then drove away with no headlights until he reached the end of the dirt road.

He failed to breathe easy until they pulled onto the expressway. What time would it be when they arrived at Eve's house?

Her head tilted to one side.

Philip smiled at the sleeping beauty. It looked as though they'd postpone the conversation about Jordan yet again. He'd forced Eve to help him and put her life in danger. He hadn't even discussed their relationship. How selfish was that? He didn't know how he would make his plan work if he lost Mr. Jacobsen's account, but he could think more clearly tomorrow. Turning off the freeway, he headed into Triville. Then he pulled onto the road leading to Eve's Clips and hit a speed bump.

Eve flinched and rubbed her eyes as Philip wheeled into her driveway, gravel crunching underneath the tires. "Where are we?"

He cut the engine then patted her shoulder. "You're home safe and sound."

Dew on the grass between the car and the porch sparkled underneath the spotlight on the corner of the house. Crickets chirping cut into the quiet night as he helped Eve from the passenger's seat. He placed his arm around her waist and they trudged to the door. "We'll see Chief Grimes tomorrow. Then you and I will talk."

"He doesn't keep office appointments on the week-ends. We'll have to wait until Monday." Eve grinned. "Unless my idea works."

"What idea?"

"I'll tell you tomorrow after church." Eve unlocked her front door.

Philip pulled her close to him and kissed her with all the strength he had left. She fell limp and laid her head on his shoulder. He stroked her hair then released her. "I'll pick you up at ten-thirty. Get some sleep."

She unlocked her door and went inside.

What plan could she possibly have? Hope trickled into his tired bones on the way to the car and he picked up his pace.

21

A buzzing racket jarred me. I reached out from under the comforter and hit the nightstand. Sleep held down my eyelids like heavy weights, but the noise repeated and blasted them open. I picked up the small, white clock, and pounded the OFF button. "You don't really want me to get up do you?"

Why was I so tired? The detective work. Philip! I sprang out of bed, went into the bathroom and splashed cold water on my face. I donned a burgundy dress and a pair of black pumps just in time to answer the doorbell. "Good morning."

"Hi, gorgeous." Weariness filled Philip's voice.

I locked the door, and we ambled out into a crisp mountain breeze and got in the car. "I kinda' hate to part with her tomorrow," Philip said as he set the motor running and backed out.

"I know."

"What's your plan?"

I couldn't have stopped my grin if I'd wanted to. Wait until he heard it. "I'll tell you as soon as we leave the service. We'll put it in motion right away."

"I'd like to know now." Philip headed into town.

I opened my mouth to tell him about my idea, but before I collected my thoughts he motored onto the steep hill to the church. The old car sputtered and rolled backward. He clenched his jaw, gripped the steering wheel with both hands, and pushed the pedal to the floor. The vehicle crept to the gravel lot. He had so much patience with the car...and soapy bubbles...and faulty hair products.

"My curiosity's killing me," he said as he cut the engine.

"I don't have time to give you all the details before church."

He sat back in his seat and gazed at me with pleading eyes.

"We'll return to the thieves' house."

He gasped.

"One of those hoods has a gun."

"Everybody here has a gun. It's a way of life."

"Do you have a gun?"

"Yes. Jordan taught me how to shoot a revolver."

"Yeah, but it's for your protection. You're not a criminal."

I pulled down my eyebrows and frowned at him. "Of course, I'm not a criminal. Have a little faith in me. My scheme will work."

"I'll listen," he said, but doubt lined his voice.

"We need to attend the service."

"You're right."

We strolled to the church and dropped down onto the nearest pew.

The choir members lined up behind us and marched down the aisle, singing. The congregation joined in, and sweet notes filled the church. The hymn ended as the songsters sat down in seats behind the altar.

Reverend Binder rose from his chair and I started going through my scheme in my mind, reassuring myself it would work and the crooks would return the money. Before I knew it, Reverend Binder mentioned the closing prayer. I realized I'd plotted the rest of the day and missed the entire sermon.

The minister held out his arms. "May the Lord bless you and keep you in His care, make his face to shine upon you, and give you peace. Amen."

Philip and I stood and waited for people to file past us before we moved outdoors to greet Reverend Binder on the rock stoop.

"Hello, Eve. Philip, it's nice to see you." He directed his gaze at me. "I hope you're showing Philip around our beautiful mountains. Today's a great day to take him on the parkway."

I tried to flash a genuine, not sheepish, grin. If he only knew where I was taking him.

Philip clasped my arm. "She's doing a good job." He set a quick pace, helped me into the passenger seat, and then scooted into his seat. "OK, out with it." He cranked the engine.

"We need to go home and change clothes. We'll dress up like college-aged kids, say nineteen."

"Why?" Philip backed out and pulled on the road. Heading downhill, they sailed past the maple and sycamore trees. "You look young enough to pull that off, but what about me?"

"Did you bring a T-shirt with a college logo? If not, stop by the drugstore and pick up one."

"I may have a Harvard jersey."

"That won't do. Buy one imprinted with Triville Community College."

Philip breezed through town and drove into my driveway. "I still don't understand. Why are we dressing like this?"

I wanted to lead him through my idea one step at a time, but apparently he wouldn't stand for that. I might as well blurt it out. "We'll saunter casually up to the criminals, tell them we lost the money, and beg them to return it."

Philip's head snapped back. You'd think I'd said we were going to Mars.

"What if they ask how much money?"

"We think it was a lot."

"They'll shoot us." Assertion lined Philip's voice.

"No. A couple kids are no threat to them."

Philip rubbed his forehead. "Why did we have the cash?"

"I've been thinking about that. A man who's isolated on a mountain asked us to take care of it for him. Doesn't that summarize what happened?"

"Hmm." Philip tilted his head and sat silent as though weighing my words while the motor idled. "Yes."

He didn't seem to grasp the brilliance of my plot. "If they feel sorry for us, they'll give it back."

"Feel sorry for us. Are you kidding?"

"Everyone has a soft spot and a good side. Most people like kids. You know how some hoodlums have boundaries. They might beat up a man their age and size, but they wouldn't harm a hair on a little kid's head." Knowing human nature was part of running a beauty shop, but apparently stockbrokers didn't have a clue about the inner workings of people's hearts and minds.

Philip thumped the steering wheel. "Now that you mention it, I've heard about prisoners turning on inmates convicted of abusing children."

"Then there was my Grandma's neighbor who robbed banks on the other side of the country. No one knew he was a thief. When he stayed gone weeks at a time, we all thought he was away on legitimate business. My grandmother baked him apple pies. He cut firewood, repaired broken windows in her house, and cleaned gutters for her."

Philip's mouth gaped. "No way?"

"Yeah. The feds caught him and put him in the local jail before they transported him to prison. While he was still here, she took him a pie!"

Philip laughed so hard he nearly hit his head on the steering wheel. "You can't be serious."

"Yes, I am."

"You're saying crooks, or at least some of them, have two sides. Even though they break the law, they might not hurt certain people because they mean something to them. We can fall into the latter category if we put on a good act, and these thieves aren't bad to the core." Philip cocked an eyebrow as though he still had doubts. Then a glint of hope flickered in his eyes telling me he liked the idea. "OK, see you soon."

I scooted out, and he drove off.

My strategy had to work.

~*~

Philip looked nineteen standing on my porch in his Bermuda shorts and a Triville Community College T-shirt. I couldn't help but laugh.

I'd put my hair in a ponytail, and he flipped it as I locked the door. "You could be in high school. I like the pink bow."

"Thank you. I need to finish your disguise."

He glanced down. "This isn't good enough?"

I shook my head. "You did a great job, but you

need more."

We entered the shop, and I motioned toward the middle salon chair. "Have a seat."

He obliged and peered in the mirror. Silky strands swished as I picked up a blond wig and placed it on his head.

"Oh no. I'm not wearing this."

I'd figured he'd fuss about it. "Yes, you have to. Sit still." I adjusted it then combed some fake hair forward.

He pushed it off his eyes. "This doesn't work. Remove it."

"I'll trim it. Be still." I picked up the scissors and Philip's brow furrowed.

I styled the wig so the bangs fell just over his eyebrows and the sides of it right above his ears. "There. When you put on sunglasses, the criminals won't see anything but your lips, nose, cheeks, and chin. Can you change your voice when you talk?"

Philip leaned forward and stared in the mirror.

I could tell by the way he eyed the new look, he was fine with it.

"That's amazing. You're talented. They'll never suspect I'm a thirty-five-year-old stockbroker." He spoke in a tone much higher pitched than usual.

I laughed. "That's great. Wear these." I handed him a large, black-rimmed pair of shades from the vanity. Then I snatched up some with red rims dotted with tiny flowers and put them on. "We're ready to go."

Philip placed his arm around my waist and guided me to the car. Then he slipped into the driver's seat. The wig didn't budge.

"Your hair's holding up well."

"I have a great hairdresser." He chuckled then he stiffened and backed out.

"We won't take chances. If I sense our act isn't working, I'll pull on your arm and say I'm late getting home to help my mom with dinner."

"We'll tell them we lost money on a dead-end road almost no one uses. How lame does that sound?" Disbelief lined Philip's voice.

"We'll say we wanted to be alone."

Philip tilted his head. "Hmm. Good idea."

"I wracked my brain coming up with it."

"I guess you're OK with this because you carry on conversations with all kinds of people all day. Do hairdressers take psychology?"

"It's not required for a license, but I actually completed several classes, because the subject interests me."

"I thought so."

I wanted Philip to be comfortable with our ruse. "I'll be able to judge how much we can say by studying the criminals' expressions and body language. If they're leaning into us, they like what they hear. If one of them turns his shoulders toward us, he really approves of what we're saying."

"It's not hard to read a fist coming at you." Philip exited the expressway and wheeled onto the road leading into Chapsburg.

I gave him a friendly jab on the arm, hoping to relax him. "They'll not hit us. We know they're thieves, but they don't realize that. I think they'll take a likin' to you."

"Yeah, right." Philip drove onto the dirt road to their house. The wooden brown structure looked weather beaten in the daylight. "Where should I park?"

"Pull off here. We'll head toward the place, poke around the bushes, and act like we're looking for something."

Philip continued a little farther. "I'll get close enough for us to run for our lives." A hint of sarcasm lined his voice. He parked in tall grass on the shoulder.

We edged out. Getting into the act right away, he swung his hand into a holly bush. "Ouch."

I took hold of it. Bright pink scratches lined the top of his skin, but there wasn't any blood. "Sorry. Try the wild azaleas." I pointed to a shrub near the house.

He pushed back some of the branches then picked a flower and handed it to me. "For my lady."

A door slammed and Philip's eyes bulged.

I touched his shoulder. "It's all right. I'll handle it."

The thieves stomped to us scowling like two angry bulldogs.

The heavier man ran his hand through greasy, medium-length blond hair. "What you kids doin' out here?" His voice sounded gruff, but our disguises had worked.

I stuck out my hand. "Hi, I'm Windy."

He shook it with an extremity that looked as though he hadn't washed in several days, his fingernails black with grease—from a stolen car, no doubt. "Joey."

"Nice to meet you. This is Charlie." I motioned toward Philip and grinned real big.

Joey pointed to the other guy. "Jack."

I waved, and Philip said, "Hello" in his high-pitched voice.

Jack grunted. "Answer the question. What ya'll

doin' out here."

Seeing them face to face in broad daylight I glimpsed the meanness in their eyes, and my courage dwindled. I swallowed hard. "We lost something."

Jack cracked his knuckles. "Way out here?"

"Yeah. We were..." I shifted my weight to cover up the shiver overtaking me and cut my gaze toward Philip. "You know."

Joey grinned. "I see. What'd you lose?"

My eyes met Joey's, and my legs turned to gelatin. "Two duffle bags. Have you seen them?"

Jack tilted his head. "What'd they look like?"

"They're black and about this wide." I held out my hands, showing a three-foot width.

"What's in them?" Joey took a step toward me.

My mouth went dry as I tried to speak.

"Something for someone else," Philip said.

"Yeah. Yeah." Joey eyed Jack as he spoke, his voice deep.

Jack nodded. "Yeah."

I glanced at Philip. He appeared calm. This was going well.

Philip clasped his hands in front of him. "We were taking money to the bank in Merchantville for a man who's isolated on a mountaintop."

Joey's mouth gaped. He stepped back, his body language telling me he didn't like what he heard. "In Merchantville. How'd you end up here?"

Philip leaned into me. "Like she said, maybe we...uh...sorta got distracted, wanted to get off the freeway." Philip gestured with his hands. "We saw this convenient side road, pulled onto it, and you know." He cocked an eyebrow. "We got outside the car and leaned our heads on the duffle bags like they were pillows."

I couldn't help but stare in amazement. If Philip ever decided to give up his job, he could be an actor.

Joey slapped his knee and laughed. "Yeah. Yeah. I guess you ain't hurtin' nothin'. Go ahead and look around. I hope you find 'em. I think you're gonna' be in trouble if you don't."

No. They had to give them to us. My mind froze. *Try to relax and think.* "You must have seen them."

Jack set his jaw firm. "No, we ain't." Anger filled his tone, and he started to walk away, Joey on his heels. Apparently, he didn't like telling me twice they hadn't seen them.

My insides shook, but I caught up to them. "Maybe they're lying around, and you just haven't noticed them."

"I told you we don't know anything about any bags. You can stay out here on the road, but don't follow us. If you do, we might have to throw you off the bridge." Jack laughed.

So much for body language. I understood the message plain and clear. "What bridge?" I wanted him to think I had no idea what he was talking about.

Joey looked over his shoulder. "You're getting too nosey. Look for your loot then leave."

They stomped back to the house and went inside.

My heart pounded so hard I thought it might jump out of my chest. "They won't give the satchels to us."

Philip wandered to the azaleas and poked around. "In case they're watching, put on a good show."

"Right." I took a stick and swished it underneath the holly bush.

We worked our way down one shrub at a time until we reached the car and climbed in.

Philip started the engine and backed out with his lips turned down.

Tears wet my eyelashes. I'd been no help at all.

"I guess I'll have to talk to Chief Grimes in the morning." Defeat lined his voice.

I slumped in my seat. "I'm sorry my plan didn't work, but I don't think Chief Grimes will announce to Triville you've lost Mr. Jacobsen's money."

Philip pulled onto the expressway. "I know he won't while he's working on the case, but what about afterward? I'll lose the account if Mr. Jacobsen thinks I'm irresponsible. I'm feeling sick."

I patted his arm. "Please don't be upset. If we explain to Robert, uh Chief Grimes, surely he'll get the cash from these gangsters and keep quiet about it. If nothing else, you'd think he'd be grateful to us for finding this den of thieves."

22

I opened my mouth, leaned over the cream-colored vanity, and smoothed on lipstick. Did the bright lights above the mirror give me a washed out look, or did thinking about the police station drain my color? There weren't any gangsters locked up there. They were in the jail. I only suggested we go because I knew how much Philip wanted us to solve this case. If he wasn't happy, I wasn't either.

The doorbell rang, and I still hadn't called Just Right about my product mix-up. What happened to my time? It would have to wait. Getting Mr. Jacobsen's investment was much more important. I hurried downstairs and answered the door. So rigid, Philip's face muscles looked as though he'd shaved in glue. I smiled, hoping to cheer him.

"Hi," he said without cracking a smile. Then he guided me to the car, my green cotton skirt swirling around my calves. There must have been something about visiting with the Chief of Police that made us dress up. Philip wore a gray suit.

We scooted into the car, and Philip hit the steering wheel with the palm of his hand. "Waiting eight days to report the missing funds puts me in a suspicious light. What was I thinking?" He backed out.

A twinge of pain twisted my heart to see Philip so distressed. "Don't worry, Robert and I grew up together. He played quarterback preceding the renowned Bullet Bounts at Triville High. He left here only to attend North Carolina State and earn a degree in public administration. When you explain what happened, he'll understand. He knows how the residents gossip." I pointed to a road just before the next stoplight. "Make a left on Dogwood Lane."

Philip switched on his blinker and turned.

"You can't change what you did eight days ago. I'm sure Robert will agree you're doing the right thing now. You'll hand over a couple car thieves. Judging from the number of stolen parts at the warehouse, they're probably part of a larger ring."

"That might make a difference." Philip wheeled into a space at the front of a huge parking lot, cut the engine, and let me out.

We climbed wide cement stairs and entered the one-story, brick building. I shivered as I passed through the metal detector. Only places with people up to no good needed such bold devices. We passed by straight chairs lining the walls on either side of the room as we walked to a police woman behind a window shielded with black bars.

"Hi, I'm Philip Wells and this is Eve Castleberry. We have an appointment with Chief Grimes."

How did I not know this lady with the round face and big blue eyes? She must've transferred from another town. I smiled at her and tried to hold my tongue, but I couldn't. "Where are you from?"

"I'm sick of telling everybody my life history." She smirked. "I'm from South Carolina. I relocated here three weeks ago. If you must know, I separated from my deadbeat husband. This place was just as good as any to move to. Nobody cares about anybody no matter where you live."

There seemed to be more than black iron bars separating us.

Philip poked his hand into the small opening between the counter and the bottom of the bars. "Philip Wells. Triville grows on you."

How kind of Philip, and his words...my heart fluttered like a humming bird. Was the dream I was too afraid to dream coming true?

She extended her chubby palm. "I'm Mary Jane. I can tell the two of you aren't criminals. I have good instincts." She pointed to a couple of chairs on the left. "Have a seat over there. He'll be right out."

I couldn't walk away without chatting, trying to make Mary Jane feel more welcome. "Eve Castleberry. Stop by Bob's Diner. I guarantee one of those nosey people will come up to your table and keep you company." I reached in my purse, pulled out a card, and laid it on the counter. "Come over to Eve's Clips, and I'll create a gorgeous "law enforcement special" hairdo for you."

She grasped it then gazed at it as though it was more than a connection to a hairdresser. "Hey thanks, I'll call tomorrow and make an appointment."

"Great." If a person wasn't a devoted Triville citizen when she moved here, we'd make one out of her.

A steel door to the right opened and Robert stuck out his head. His dark hair color and athletic build remained the same as they had been in high school. "Eve Castleberry, why would you need to see me in a business capacity?" He sounded friendly, but confused.

"This is my friend, Philip Wells."

Robert gave Philip a robust handshake. "So you're

the guy Eve's been hanging out with at the diner. It's good to meet you in person. Here to see Mr. Jacobsen, aren't you?"

Philip's eyes snapped wide. "Yes."

Everybody here knew everyone else's business, and I thought by now Philip realized that. Of course, the police chief in New York probably wouldn't have such information.

We followed Robert through the doorway. The lock clicking behind us reminded me I trod where hoodlums passed, and I stiffened. Philip took my arm as Robert escorted us to the first cubicle on the right. A picture of Jewel, his wife, sat on his mahogany desk. Seeing her image made the surroundings seem more familiar, and some of my anxiety dissipated.

"Have a seat."

We sat down on two chrome chairs as Robert sank into a black leather office chair. He pushed strands of hair off his forehead. "What's up?"

"Two things. Philip had a little trouble about a week ago. We looked into the problem ourselves." The muscles in Robert's face tightened, and his irritated expression jarred my nerves. I crossed my legs and slung my dangling foot back and forth. "I know we shouldn't have, but we thought we could handle it."

"What kind of trouble?" He leaned forward.

"Let me finish first. While taking care of Philip's situation, we ran across a car theft ring."

Robert's mouth gaped. "You what?"

I'm sure he couldn't imagine how I'd done such a thing. My stomach churned, but I had to make him understand the entire situation.

"Start from the beginning."

"All right." I took a deep breath.

"I'm listening. Take your time." He leaned back.

"You know how everyone noses into everybody else's business in Triville."

"Yes."

"It's extremely important to Philip that no one discuss this problem."

Robert sat straight up. "For crying out loud, Eve. What is it?"

The tone of his voice sounded the same as when we were in high school and I'd accidentally made a date with someone who wasn't Jordan. I'd asked Robert to help me solve the dilemma. I recalled that he thought I should've had better sense. I went mute.

Philip scooted his chair close to the desk and looked Robert straight in the eyes. "Someone stole Mr. Jacobsen's money."

"I see." Robert drew out his words. Then he asked, "Eight days ago?"

I held in a gasp of disbelief.

"Yes. How did *you* know exactly when the theft occurred?" Philip's voice sounded matter-of-fact, but he peered at Robert with wide unbelieving eyes.

Robert tapped his forefinger on his lips. "Just say it was a lucky guess. I assume Corley gave it to you to invest, so what happened next? What did you do with it?"

If I knew Robert, he had a reason for answering Philip's question with questions.

"I drove to the motel, went inside, and laid it on the bed while I arranged my flight to New York. Then, I slipped into the bathroom. Without sleeping, I flew home to put the money in a bank. When I reached my condo and opened the satchels, they held only toilet paper. I went numb. The words *Get back the investment* screamed in my head, and I could hardly think straight. I took the first plane out of New York to Merchantville. Eve and I figured whoever swiped the cash made the switch at the motel."

"Ah. Hmm. That makes sense." Robert's eyes held a look of satisfaction as though he was convinced he was right about something. "What's this about a car theft ring?"

Philip pressed his lips into a straight line and gazed at me.

This was the perfect time to use our leverage. "Promise us you won't say anything about Mr. Jacobsen's missing cash. If he hears Philip lost it, he'll drop his account..." I bit my bottom lip "...at best. He might even sue Philip. No one knows it's gone except us and the thieves who took it."

Robert's eyebrows shot up.

"I know how people make deals with law enforcement, so I figured you and I go way back. We're friends, right?"

"Yes, we are." Robert's voice sounded calm and steady.

"I thought if we told you where to find the car thieves, you'd get Mr. Jacobsen's cash when you arrest them and give it to Philip."

"I'll look into your accusation. That's what policemen do. We catch the bad men and take care of the good guys." Authority rang in Robert's voice.

"Can you just give the cash to Philip and not tell the newspaper or anyone else?"

"That's *not* how we do things."

I wasn't asking for a crash course in criminology. I glared at Robert.

"I have to verify it belongs to Philip via Mr.

Jacobsen. Then, with luck, the local district attorney will say it's all right to give it back."

Philip scooted to the edge of his seat. "I can't tell Mr. Jacobsen. That's why we found the creeps instead of coming to you in the first place." Fear and pleading lined his voice.

Had Robert paid no attention to anything I'd said? I wanted to stand up and shake him.

He reached for a legal pad on his desk and picked up a pen then handed the items to Philip. "Give me the exact amount of money and denominations. Describe the packaging. Were the bills marked? Tell me anything and everything you remember."

Philip started writing.

Robert directed his gaze at me. "You should have come to me to start with." A tinge of anger lined his voice.

"We know that. That's why we're here now." My voice had an edge to it, and I didn't care. I'd helped take care of his little girl, Annie, when Jewel had to return to the hospital not long after she was born, and Jordan had built the nursery.

Robert relaxed his broad shoulders. "I believe I can recover the money."

His words blew me away. "We haven't told you where the thieves are."

Robert picked up another pad and pencil. "I don't think the car thieves you found have Mr. Jacobsen's money, but I'm very interested in their whereabouts. If they're the two I'm thinking of, they're career criminals and extremely dangerous."

I nearly fell off my chair. "Who do you think stole Mr. Jacobsen's money?"

"I'll let you know. Give me the information you

have on the car theft ring."

At least he appeared to be connecting with me. He made notes as I told him about the two strangers we'd followed from the diner while Philip continued to write on the pad.

"Whew." Robert put down his pencil and rubbed his forehead. "Don't go back over there. It's a wonder they didn't kill you. If they'd seen you around that big warehouse, you wouldn't be sitting here now." His voice was like iron.

I shook inside. "No, we won't."

Robert had the same look on his face in eleventh grade when I told him Jewel had eyed a necklace with a heart-shaped dangle, and he should purchase it for her birthday. My skin tingled with excitement. "This is important information, isn't it?"

"You know me too well. I'll be straight with you. The FBI's been after Joey Hargrove and Jack "Redhead" Climmer for years. They're part of a large, multi-state operation stealing cars in North Carolina, Virginia, and South Carolina. The Feds will be glad to have this." Robert patted the notepad. "I'll give the information to them right away. I'll probably assist with the operation." He puffed out his chest, and I knew the significance of what I'd just told him. I wasn't about to leave without a commitment. "So, you'll call us to pick up Mr. Jacobsen's cash?"

"If Philip's notes match the details of the money, and *if* my plan works, I'll do that and not reveal Philip and Mr. Jacobsen's names to the newspaper, or tell anyone outside the courts. That's the best I can offer. The important word is *if*."

Philip handed Robert the pad.

"Coming from you, that's enough. Thank you."

Robert was great at his job, and his word was as reliable as the sun coming up each morning.

"You're welcome."

We stood, and Robert accompanied us to the steel door and held it open.

But when would he call about the money? And who stole it if it wasn't the two car thieves?

23

I bumped into a large concrete planter with pink azalea bushes next to the cement steps outside the police station. "Ouch."

Philip guided me across the asphalt parking lot.

"Let's stop a second." I bent to massage my shin then hobbled to the car. "Robert will help us."

"I hope you're right." Philip's lips turned down as he opened the door for me.

"Don't you believe me?"

He cocked an eyebrow. "Of course, that's what you know in your heart, but I need to hold the cash in my hands." He scooted in and rubbed his hand along the steering wheel. "Want to go with me to turn 'er in?" A hint of melancholy lined his voice.

"Sure."

He drove to Lloyd's garage in silence, pulled up and parked. "She's dependable." He patted the dashboard.

"Great for detective work."

"I can't believe we thought those car thieves wanted by the F.B.I. took Mr. Jacobsen's money." Philip laughed. "The way Jack and Joey kept looking at each other when we asked about it."

I chuckled.

"No wonder they didn't offer to give us the money." Philip guffawed. "Not that they would've if they'd had it. I'm glad we found them though. I think

Chief Grimes appreciated our help." Hope rang in his voice.

I stopped snickering. "For sure. I've known Robert a long time. The look on his face when he talked about Jack and Joey...umm. He wants those guys. He's probably on the phone with the feds right now."

"Maybe he will work out his plan and give me the money." Philip rubbed his palms together. "Let's go in and pick up the other car." He scooted out and opened the passenger door then put his arm around my waist. "How's your shin?"

"Much better, thank you." We wandered into the repair side of Lloyd's, the smell of motor oil greeting us.

Three cars sat in the service line in the back. Lloyd wrote on a paper at the tall desk at the front. He grinned and touched the ends of his dark hair. "I know. I haven't called. It's been busy."

"You're still handsome. Make an appointment when you can."

"OK." Lloyd pulled back his shoulders and looked toward Philip. "Let me get the key from you."

Philip pulled it out of his pants pocket and gave it to him. "That's quite a car. At first I thought it might stop on me for good."

Lloyd added the key to a pegboard over his desk. "Yeah. The girl has a few kinks I haven't ironed out. It's always on loan, but I'm glad you enjoyed driving her. If we can settle up, I'll call for the rental that tore up on you."

Philip and Lloyd made the transaction. Then Lloyd picked up the in-house phone. "Bring up the dark blue sedan."

It blazed into the left lane and stopped. The driver,

who wore a blue shirt with Elmer stitched on the pocket, grinned as he turned the key fob over to Philip.

"Thanks, buddy." Philip said. Then he and I got in the car. "Want to celebrate with lunch at Bob's Diner?" he asked as he pulled onto Main Street.

"Absolutely. Then we can have brownies for dessert at my place."

"Now, that's a party."

We sailed up the hill, parked, and entered the restaurant to the aroma of fresh brewed coffee and cheeseburgers.

"How ya'll doin'?" Bonnie Sue said from behind the counter. "Just sit anywhere. I'll be right over." She winked at Philip.

He gave her a half smile as I plunked down in the first booth facing the entrance.

Philip sat across from me, grabbed a menu from between the mustard and ketchup bottles, and peered at it.

"Look at your lap. Quick."

Philip moved as though he intended to turn around.

"Don't."

"Why?"

My nerves vibrated as I rummaged in my purse for a pen. I snatched a napkin out of the holder, scribbled Jack and Joey, and shoved it across the table with a shaky hand.

Philip slumped in his seat.

Jack and Joey leaned against the wall beside the shelf where the cook set to-go orders. In my mind I heard Robert saying they would've shot us if they'd seen us. I trembled in my seat. They were free in the woods they lived in now, but not for long. "They're getting take-out. We're all right." I spoke so softly I barely heard my words, but Philip nodded.

Jack meandered toward us.

My hands grew sweaty. Lowering my head, I pretended to search in my pocketbook. "Look at the wall."

Philip moved his entire body away from the aisle.

I caught a glimpse of Jack headed toward the men's room.

Bonnie Sue sashayed over. "Sorry I kept you waiting. What can I bring you, handsome?"

"Cheeseburger and a soda." Philip mumbled without even glancing up.

Her lips turned down. "What about you?" She stared at me with puzzled green eyes.

Having Jack and Joey so close gave me the willies, and it was hard to think. Without considering the menu I said, "I'll have the same. Thank you."

Jack headed to the check-out counter, but Bonnie Sue shielded us from his sight. Joey squinted and looked our way. My heart skipped a beat. I could only hope he checked out Bonnie Sue? Bonnie Sue. What would cheer her up? "It's been a difficult morning for him." I nodded toward Philip.

She put her hand on her hip. "At least you're friendly. Why are the two of you scrunched down like turtles?"

Could the seat swallow me? "Just tired."

"All right. I'll get this out right away."

Joey picked up a to-go bag. Then they left.

My muscles relaxed. "Whew!" I let out a big sigh. "They're gone."

Philip sat up. "Yeah. Soon they'll be gone for a long time, and the world will be a better place."

"I can't help but wonder why they're hanging around Triville. Do you think they're planning to steal from Lloyd's garage? In addition to the rental service, he also has a few new vehicles for sale."

Philip held up his hand. "Whoa. We need to let Chief Grimes take care of those creeps from now on. He knows they're staking out something in the area. He'll put it all together. Whatever it is."

"That's true."

"You've done enough sleuthing. Your shop's in order. You can go back to rolling up hair."

"Yeah, but I can't stop thinking about the case. I've worked hard to solve it. My inner detective's on alert."

Philip laughed loud.

Bonnie Sue set Philip's plate in front of him, wrinkles creasing her brow.

"Thank you." Philip flashed her a big grin.

Her eyes lit up. "You're welcome, handsome." She served my cheeseburger then strutted off with her signature wiggle.

I picked up a French fry. "You took care of that."

"I don't want to hurt anyone's feelings. She's just kidding around." Philip sipped his sweet tea.

"I know."

He swallowed a bite of his burger. "Chief Grimes led us to believe he knows something about Mr. Jacobsen's money. I don't understand how that's possible. Do you think that's true?"

"Oh, yeah. He's very good at his job. He's had offers to work for Homeland Security, but he loves Triville. I can't think of anyone I'd rather have solving a crime."

"I'll hold onto that thought until he hands me the cash." Philip wiped his mouth and laid down his napkin. "With Chief Grimes in charge there's no need for us, especially you, to be involved anymore."

Bonnie Sue brought the bill and winked at Philip when she laid it on the table.

He fished five dollars out of his wallet for her then we stood. Philip paid at the register and we left. In moments we sat in the sedan, Philip cranking the engine. "That was a close call with those two hoodlums. The sooner Robert locks them up the better."

"Amen, to that."

Philip drove down the mountain and pulled onto the road leading to Eve's Clips. "Theft aside, I've come to like it here."

My pulse quickened, his words still spinning in my head when he parked in my driveway. I let us inside, and we proceeded to the kitchen.

"Have a seat. How about coffee to go with the brownies?"

He pulled a chair up and gazed at me. "Yes, having a cup of your coffee soothes a troubled spirit."

"Huh?"

"I was thinking about the day I met you. You stopped what you were doing to bring me a drink after the crash."

I reached in the cabinet for a porcelain tray and arranged the brownies. The fact he remembered sent a warm tingle up my spine, but I didn't want him to feel indebted. I turned and placed napkins on the table. "Anyone in Triville would have done the same." I snickered. "Except Bonnie Sue. For you, she would have baked sweet rolls too."

His lips turned up and his gaze softened. "Your Triville hospitality may endear you to me, but that's only part of it. You're a gifted woman."

"I'm glad you think so. I'm just an ordinary hairstylist getting by day to day as best I can." The coffee maker gurgled as I set down the dessert. "Have a brownie while we wait on the drinks."

He reached for one, broke off a bite, and popped it in his mouth. "Hmm. You're such a good cook. That's only one of your talents. I've never known anyone who understands people as well as you."

"All hair dressers worth a flip understand people. Our customers expect it. Mostly, I listen. While I'm working on my customers' hair they talk about their troubles. While hashing them over aloud, they usually solve them on their own." The coffee maker cut off, and I served our drinks before plopping down next to Philip.

"I'd like to hear about Jordan." A caring tone lined his voice.

My stomach clenched. "I wouldn't know where to start."

He scooted his chair closer and hugged me. "I understand Jordan will always have a place in your heart. I'd never want to change that. I want to learn about him because he played such an important part in your life, and I care about you so much. How did you two meet?"

His words gave me hope the two of us might have a serious relationship, and his touch gave me courage. Was it enough to trust him and leave the details of the distance between us to God? Ever since Mr. Jacobsen brought up the subject of my late husband I'd owed Philip an explanation. I set down my coffee and leaned back in my seat. "It's hard to say how old we were. Our parents used to visit each other when we were toddlers, so we definitely went way back." I chuckled at the fond memory and to cover up my nervousness. "In our earliest interaction Jordan pulled my pigtails in kindergarten." I couldn't help but smile. "But...he wouldn't let anyone else pull them."

"When did you begin dating?"

"Near the end of our freshman year in high school he invited me to parties. Our sophomore year we went out alone. From then on, it was Jordan and me. We attended football games, spring festivals, everything high school kids do. A couple of my classmates didn't have steady boyfriends. They always worried if anyone would ask them to prom, or if they should attend a get-together alone. For as long as I can remember, Jordan was there for me."

Talking about Jordan drained me. Should I tell Philip that Jordan's death tore out my heart, and I hadn't been the same since? I looked at life through skewed lenses now. Nothing was in focus. Tears welled up in my eyes, but I blinked them back. I had loved Jordan with all my being, but I cared about Philip. Where did my feelings for him come from? How could I explain? I didn't understand myself.

"I can't even imagine how hard it's been for you to have someone who meant so much taken away. It's clear Jordan loved you very much. If he could be with you he would, but he can't. I can't take his place, don't even want to try, but I do want to be with you a lot. I'm not moving to Rhode Island. If everything works out with Mr. Jacobsen, I'll file a request to start a Western North Carolina Make More Money Branch and live in Triville."

Had I heard him correctly? My breath hitched when I tried to speak. "Are you serious?"

"Yes. I love you, and I love it here."

I tingled from my head to my toes. "I never imagined you'd want to be in Triville permanently. It must be so different from New York, your home."

"It is. I'll take you there one day."

"I'd love that. Uh, to visit."

Philip picked up his coffee and sipped. "Just one more question. Then I'll let you share things about Jordan when and if you want to. I'll always want to hear them."

What would Jordan think about my talking to Philip about him? Words stuck in my throat. "What else did you want to know?"

"What happened to Jordan?"

Remembering pierced my heart as though someone stabbed it with a knife. "Jordan ran a branch office of a health insurance company. I don't think I told you that. He awoke early and worked out at the gym three days a week before he went to his job, but he'd taken the day off. That morning he left to drive two hundred miles to see his mother for her birthday. She had moved to help take care of Jordan's sister's children." I swallowed hard. "Well, you probably didn't want to know that."

"I want to know everything you'd like to tell me." Philip's eyes looked caring, concerned.

"He stopped at the intersection of Main Street and Hill Road. That's the one that goes to Bob's Diner. His light turned green, and he pulled forward."

Philip nodded.

"This drunken jerk driving a semi-truck came barreling through the red light, smashed into the driver's side of Jordan's car, and killed him." I thought I would die after the words came out of my mouth. I'd not said that out loud to anyone, not my mother, not my friends, no one. I doubled over and nearly fell forward.

Philip put me on his lap and enveloped me in his arms. I cried. My mom had visited and helped with Jordan's arrangements after he was killed. I'd shed tears then, but not too many, because I loved her, and she was recovering from cancer treatments. At Jordan's funeral I sniffled, but I didn't want to break down in front of the whole town.

When I left the grave, Joyce Westmoreland drove me home. Mary Lou Griffith and Loraine Peters accompanied us. They took turns staying with me two nights each. On the seventh day, a Tuesday, I thought it best to go to work rather than sit in the house alone. I'd done that ever since. I prepared my meals, slept as well as I could, and styled my customers' hair because that was what I should do. Life went on. It had gone on without me. I was crying my heart out on Philip's shoulder. Of all the people who loved and cared about me, why Philip?

Then I knew. I didn't have to be strong for him. He was here for me. I went limp in his arms, the room spinning, weakness sweeping over me. He carried me to the living room sofa and wiped my tears with his thumb. I cried until I couldn't cry anymore, and Philip held me close.

When I finally stopped, I felt exposed, naked, but it didn't matter. For the first time since Jordan died, I was free to be me. I knew then I'd always love Jordan. There'd always be a place in my heart he filled no one else could enter, but I had a big heart. When Jordan died, my love hadn't run out like water from a glass. It had been there all along, waiting for the right person to tap into it.

Philip brushed my hair back from my face.

I gazed up at him, knowing my eyes must be swollen and look awful. "Are you seriously thinking of moving to Triville?"

"Yes. I've been researching the surrounding area every night. I have ideas for the Western North Carolina Branch of Make More Money. As soon as I get my hands on Mr. Jacobsen's funds, I'll propose my plan to George and ask for permission to set it up." Philip's lips turned down. "But I need that money ASAP."

24

Tuesday morning the sun shone in the window creating a stripe on the beige carpet almost as bright as the glow burning in me. I flipped back the comforter with such vigor it fell in the floor.

Thoughts of attending hair styling demonstrations in shops with mirrored walls and modern art danced in my head as I dressed in a pair of black pants and a white shirt. My customers would have the best hairdos from New York, Hollywood, and Paris. Pride for the fine shop Jordan built and all the classes I'd taken swelled in my chest as I padded down the hall to the kitchen. I brewed coffee, browned toast, and munched breakfast. A sweet strawberry aroma tantalized my nose as I took the last bite.

Finally, I had time to call Just Right Products. I darted to the shop, sat in the chair at my desk and punched in the number.

"Just Right Products. Amy speaking." I flinched at the harshness in the woman's gruff tone.

"May I speak with someone in customer service please?"

"You'll have to fill out a form."

"I need help now."

"Yes, ma'am, we can better serve you if you fill out our papers and sign them."

Why was she being difficult? Heat crawled up my neck. "My products are all mixed up. Could someone please speak to me about that?"

"I understand. Give me your address. I'll mail you the documents for reimbursement and complaints."

Had she heard anything I'd said? "If you send me papers to fill out, I have to wait to receive them, answer the questions, and return them. It could take a couple of weeks." My nerves vibrated, but I attempted to remain calm.

"I just make certain you get them. I can't control how long you keep them. Once they're in the hands of customer service they're processed in the order in which they arrived."

I held out the phone and stared at it. "Please connect me to a customer service representative now."

"Ma'am, do you want the forms or not?"

"Am I conversing with a person?"

"Yes, ma'am. I told you. I'm Amy. I'm getting another call. Please have a nice day." She hung up.

How in the world could a phone conversation make a person tremble inside? Why was this lady, uh, Amy, treating me like this? I dialed the number again.

"Just Right Products, this is Amy."

"I'd like to cancel my account with Just Right Products."

"Hold on, ma'am. I'll connect you to one of our customer service representatives."

"Good morning, This is Louise, how may I help you?"

Finally, someone pleasant. Apparently, I hadn't sounded angry enough the first time I called, or I hadn't known the magic words. "Hi, this is Eve Castleberry. I need to cancel my account with Just Right Products."

"I'm sorry you aren't pleased with our wonderful

hair products and service. If something has gone wrong, I'm here to straighten it out for you. What's your problem?" Honey dripped from the phone.

Perhaps Louise would make things right. "Several months ago I received a permanent with no neutralizer. I called and another of your customer service representatives said it was a slip up at the factory. She told me Just Right would straighten it out..."

"Yes, ma'am, I apologize. We send out thousands of supplies each day. Every once in a while something's bound to go wrong. Why don't I do this? I'll ship you ten permanents for free. How does that sound?" The tone of her voice told me she thought she'd solved my dilemma.

If she'd let me finish explaining before she'd jumped into the conversation, she'd have known why that wouldn't work. "That's a generous offer, but it's happened again. This time I received shampoo in my conditioner bottles, all of my dyes were fire engine red, and the permanent kits had no neutralizer."

"I understand, ma'am. Give me your account number, name, address, and phone number. I'll check into this and get back to you. We at Just Right Products want to make things just right for you." She practically sang the words "Just Right."

I was about ready to give up on Just Right Products and buy all my supplies online, but I gave Louise the information she requested because she was pleasant. Still after I hung up, the conversations with Amy and Louise swirled in my head.

Joyce entered carrying a white and red purse.

"Good morning. Remember I owe you a free "'do". What would you like today?" Seeing Joyce only heightened my anger at Just Right Products, but I blocked them out. I had to give her the best hairstyle ever.

She waved her hand in front of her face. "*Pff.* I'll not hold you to that. I was so glad when you called and said you weren't closing." Joyce dropped down into the chair in front of the shampoo bowl, and I leaned her back.

"I'll give you soft curls around your face."

"You've been fixing my hair for ten years, and it's always turned out great. Well, just that one tiny incident, but we won't mention that." Joyce's voice trailed off.

I poured shampoo into my hand and scrubbed. Seeing her blonde locks brought visions of white suds creeping over the floor rushing to my mind. I cringed as I applied the conditioner for bleached hair from the drugstore. The smooth, creamy liquid did the job without a hitch. Everything was fine. "There. Your hair's clean and soft."

Joyce stood, proceeded to the middle station, and sat down. Then she ran her hand through her locks. "Nice."

I parted her tresses in sections, unclipped one, held my razor at an angle and started my trim.

She directed her gaze at my reflection in the mirror as I repeated the process. "How's your new guy, Philip, right?"

No end to it. I didn't mind so much anymore. If what Philip said about moving to Triville were true, he might be my guy. "He's fine." I finished the cut, blew her hair dry, and gave her the hand mirror. She looked so cute, especially compared to her last visit.

Her face lit up. "This is great! I love it!"

"I'm so glad. As I said, it's on the house. A deal's a deal."

She stood, grabbed her purse, and pulled out a twenty. She slapped it down beside a hairbrush and laid her hand on top of it. "Eve, darlin,' you may keep me from paying full price, but you can't keep me from giving you a nice tip. You were brought up better than to turn down a gift."

I hugged her. "Thanks."

"You're welcome."

Joyce left with a spring in her step.

I straightened the station, swept up the hair around it, and plopped down at my desk. No one until two-thirty, but the vacancies were understandable. I'd just finished working long hours to give a new "'do" to every customer who hadn't been able to come because of the repairs and product problems. The thought of relaxing in the house pulled me out the door.

Philip drove up, waved from the car then sprang out. "How's it going?"

"Pretty good. How about you?"

"It's better now. I get to see you." He gave me a hug and his aftershave tickled my nostrils, a manly aroma with a hint of sweet. Just like him.

"I called Just Right Products. Someone will contact me."

Philip raised his eyebrows. "You need to resolve this now. Let's buy take-out for lunch then research beauty supply stores while we eat."

I didn't hold out much hope for Just Right Products either. "Thanks. I wanted to ask you about something else too."

"Fire away." He helped me in the passenger's seat, plunked down on the driver's side, and headed to the drugstore.

"A hairstylist show in New York sounds wonderful after we recover Mr. Jacobsen's money and find me a new supplier. Would you show me around?"

Philip's blue eyes lit up as he pulled into the parking lot and cut the engine. "Yes, I could take you to the Empire State Building, and a Broadway play too. We'd have a great time." Philip's jaw tightened. "We'll get to the bottom of the product problem this afternoon."

The faulty Just Right supplies grated on my nerves. Guilt still plagued me over using drugstore brands, but either I did that or risked creating a hair disaster.

Philip got out of the car and stuck his head inside. "I'll run in and pick up sandwiches and sodas."

"Thank you. I'd like a pimento cheese on rye. We don't need anything to drink. I have sweet tea."

Philip shut the door and left. If he said he would get to the root of a problem, he would. A few weeks ago I never would have dreamed I'd meet someone like him. I was so lonely, going through the motions of living, forcing one foot in front of the other, and I didn't even realize it. It was just my life.

Some days I'd wanted to burst into tears, and I didn't know why. It was as though sorrow lived deep inside me, then suddenly it erupted for no particular reason. I'd left that dark place filled with nothing but fog and rain and burst into a sunny yard with flowers blooming and birds singing. God was so good. He'd help us get Mr. Jacobsen's cash back and fix my problems too.

Philip opened the car door and handed me a sack. "Mandy says hello." He started the engine, drove to the house, and parked.

The dogwood tree full with spring's white blossoms and the pink azaleas stood out as though I saw them in 3-D for the first time this season. "I'll bring my laptop from the shop."

I stopped by the salon, picked up the computer, met him at my front door, and unlocked it with my free hand. We proceeded to the kitchen and placed everything on the table. I poured our tea while Philip pulled up two chairs, placing them side by side.

He sat down, bit into his turkey on rye, a distant look in his blue eyes. "How do you think someone snuck in my room and put toilet paper in those duffle bags?"

"There's only one way in." I joined him.

Philip shook his head. "Obviously, I didn't put the bolt lock on the door when I went inside to the bathroom. Every time I think about that I get so angry at myself."

"You're only human." I hugged him.

"After Mr. Jacobsen gave me the cash, I was in such a hurry. All I thought about was keeping it safe, and I did just the opposite." Philip lowered his head.

"It's all right. Robert will recover Mr. Jacobsen's money. He'll handle everything and no one will ever know the cash went missing."

Philip's lips thinned to a straight line. "I don't see how he'll do that."

"I don't know how. I just know he will. He's so smart. I've often wondered if he's an undercover agent disguised as a mild, mannered, small-town Chief of Police."

Philip stopped eating, his fork in midair.

I laughed. "I'm kidding."

"Just so he gives me the cash. He can be anything he wants." Philip finished his sandwich, put mine and his trash in the garbage can, and sat back down in front of the computer. He rubbed his hands together. "We'll find a new supplier for you right now." A few clicks echoed in the room then suddenly names of wholesalers filled the screen. He turned the laptop to face me. "Scroll down and make a few selections."

My cell phone rang. *Just Right Products.* I couldn't answer fast enough. "Eve Castleberry."

"Hi, this is Ernest Goddard at Just Right Products. I have your file and wanted to go over a few things with you. First, tell me which products were mixed up."

I repeated the information I'd given Louise about the conditioner, the dye, and the permanents.

"I see. I'm sorry that happened. Which of our salesmen calls on you?"

Unbelievable. They didn't even know who had my account? "Durbin Brown."

"Hmm. I see Les Shepherd, who handled your needs for years, retired. We don't have anyone named Durbin Brown in our sales database. How long has this man serviced your account?"

I stopped breathing as disbelief filled every fiber of my being. "A couple months. Did you say he doesn't work for you?"

"Yes, ma'am. He's not one of our employees."

"He fills out forms that say Just Right Products and takes my money."

"I understand. Anyone can print the words Just Right Products on a piece of paper. Of course, it's illegal, and we will look into it, but back to your situation. It's a horrible oversight on our part, but we have overlooked Eve's Clips and haven't assigned anyone to your shop. I can't tell you how sorry I am. I hope you'll give us another chance. I'd like to send Les's nephew, Andrew Shepherd, to call on you if you'll let me."

Words stuck in my throat. Finally, I spit out, "Uh, yes, sure. Andrew can drop by."

Who was Durbin Brown?

25

I cut off the cell phone. My head spun, Phillip and the kitchen blurring for a few seconds.

Philip stared at me with a puzzled gaze. "You're as white as New York snow. What did he say?"

"They don't have a salesman named Durbin Brown."

Philip's lips parted. "Bottles of shampoo, conditioner, and dye inside the packages—are they sealed?"

I had to think for a minute. "No. Maybe. The permanents were all sealed."

"We've been so focused on finding supplies that work. We haven't paid enough attention to the packaging." Philip shook his head. "If the culprit un-wrapped the boxes and took out the Just Right bottles, he could've switched them, or in the case of the neutralizer, removed them, and resealed the containers. He probably did, but how did he obtain them?" Wrinkles creased Philip's brow. "Tell Chief Grimes. Isn't this a crime?"

"It doesn't matter whether it is or not. If I ask Robert to look into it, he will. He hates injustice, but I don't want to distract him until he's returned Mr. Jacobsen's money."

Philip cocked an eyebrow. "I see what you mean, but we need to untangle this problem, pardon the pun."

"I believe Les's nephew will right this situation, but someone needs to put a stop to Durbin's shenanigans. What else is he up to? After Robert calls you about Mr. Jacobsen's cash, I'll tell him Durbin Brown is a fraud."

"You shouldn't have to wait," Philip said.

"No worries. It'll keep." I glanced at the clock. "I need to go back to work. It's almost time for Reverend Binder's wife."

Philip scooped my computer into the case, followed me to the shop, and placed the laptop on my desk. "I'll give you a call around five-thirty. Maybe we can grab a bite to eat somewhere and talk."

"OK."

He left and Nancy entered.

She had short black hair, blue eyes, and the most caring spirit I'd ever known. I often wondered how she did it day after day. Occasionally Reverend Binder took snippets of his sermon to explain Nancy's hard work on a project at church or at home. That was his way of telling us we shouldn't put any more pressure on her. Both of them accepted the congregants with our good and bad sides and made us feel loved. We tried to follow their examples.

"We're giving you a cut today, right?"

She touched her split ends as she dropped down into the shampoo chair. "Yes. It's getting straggly and hard to fix."

I washed her hair, tapped the conditioner, and an image of Durbin flashed in my head. I wanted to shake him. Why had he tried to destroy my business, calling on me when he didn't even work for Just Right Products? I rinsed Nancy's hair. Thanks to Smitty's Drugstore products, it was soft to the touch and the residue settled in the sink as it should. I towel-dried her locks and she made a beeline to the salon chair.

"Is there anything in particular you'd like today?" I placed my hands on the back of the seat.

"Take off about a quarter-inch, brush it back on the sides, and leave bangs in the front." She eyed herself in the mirror. "Maybe fluff it up a little at the crown."

"That will look cute on you." Following her directions, I snipped her hair. Over the noise blowing it dry, I thought I heard the door shut and peeked over my shoulder.

A harried-looking Philip charged inside. Odd. He'd said he would call. "I'm sorry. I didn't mean to barge in."

Nancy turned around and grinned real big. "Why, you're not disrupting a thing. Eve's almost finished with my hairdo."

Philip sat while I put the last touches on Nancy's style and passed her the hand mirror. She viewed the new "'do" from all directions, her eyes soft with an approving look. Then she paid and left.

Philip jumped up. "Chief Grimes wants to see me in the morning. He's giving me all of the missing money."

Joy ran through every bone in my body. I dashed to the desk and flipped the page on my appointment book. "What time?"

"Around ten to ten-thirty."

"That works. I don't have anyone until after lunch."

"Great. We'll go together. How about dinner?"

I opened my mouth to say yes, but Ellie Ringgold burst into the shop, huffing and puffing. "Chief Grimes is going to arrest your salesman, Durbin Brown. We're all gonna' watch."

"What?" I couldn't help but stare at Ellie.

Philip focused on her. "Did Chief Grimes send invitations to the capture?"

Ellie swung her yellow-flowered purse at him. "Of course not. Smitty was over at the jail delivering Robert's sinus medicine. He overheard Robert telling the secretary at the police station where he was going. Then Smitty called and told me." Ellie tapped me on the arm. "Durbin is involved in corporate espion- something...it's illegal."

Philip put his hand to his mouth. "Espionage."

"I lay you ten-to-one he messed up your products," Ellie said.

"Well, how does everybody know to go to the motel? Which one is it?"

Ellie puffed out her chest. "I started a phone tree. He's holed up at the Triville Motel where you're staying."

"I just learned he doesn't work for Just Right. How did he know about Eve's Clips?" I asked.

"Oooh." Ellie drew out the word. "He's assisting Styles by Carlton, a big beauty shop chain trying to move into all the small towns in North Carolina, South Carolina, and Georgia, and take the hairstylists' business. They have a mole inside Just Right Products. He stole the products for Durbin, the boxes, shampoo, dye—everything he needed. Then he supplied details about the shops." Ellie tilted her head. "Obviously, yours included."

I recalled how close I'd come to putting out that CLOSED sign for good and weakness swept over me. I plopped down in the chair at the shampoo bowl.

"So far three shops have gone belly-up due to their shenanigans, one in each state." Ellie waved her arm. "Come on. Follow me. We'll miss the action."

Philip pulled me up. We followed Ellie outside, hurried into the rental car, and headed down Main Street to the motel, where we joined a huge crowd standing shoulder to shoulder outside room 103, must have been nearly everyone in Triville. Philip craned his neck in the direction of the commotion.

Lloyd banged on the room door with his large hand, the short sleeves on his blue work shirt billowing in the May breeze. "Get out here, you scum. What do you mean switching Eve's products?"

Joyce Westmoreland hollered. "Yeah, I had to go to work with a wretched hairdo because of you. I looked as if I'd stuck my finger in a live electrical socket." She glanced over at me. "No offense, Eve."

Ellie screamed, "You haven't heard anything yet. Get out here and face us like a man. You rat."

The door cracked. "So I mixed up a few products. What's the crime in that?" Durbin's voice wafted outside, the cockiness gone from it.

Bonnie Sue sashayed to the front of everyone. "We have a hairicide law in Triville, and you broke it. You killed a lot of perfectly good hairdos. Out, or we'll come in and get you."

Durbin stuck out his nose.

"All the way." Mandy Hawkins's harsh voice rang out.

Durbin edged out wearing nothing but a white T-shirt and a pair of red boxer shorts with big white polka dots, his spindly legs sticking out like toothpicks.

I snickered. I was so glad he would never call on me again.

Chief Grimes pulled up, lights flashing and his siren blasting over the roar of laughter filling the parking lot.

Robert jumped out of the car, and I recognized his fake serious look from grammar school. With his jaw set firm he approached the crowd. The giveaway was the mischievous look dancing in his eyes. I'd seen it many times when he'd told me later he'd been laughing inside.

"Move back. Out of the way, please." He passed through the gawkers to the motel, handcuffed Durbin, and dragged him off. Putting his hand over Durbin's head so it cleared the top of the door frame, he stuffed him in the backseat of the police car then got in and drove off.

The Triville residents disbursed, laughing and clapping.

Ellie sidled over to me and Philip. "Now aren't you glad I came to get you?"

I gave her a bear hug.

Philip shook her hand. "I wouldn't have missed it. Thank you."

~*~

The next morning I sat beside Philip in front of Chief Grimes' mahogany desk, the sun seeping through the small window behind us onto a stack of papers. Two laundry bags that appeared to be stuffed with money rested on the top shelf of a wooden bookcase on the back wall. The urge to meander over and snatch them pulled at me like a magnet.

Philip patted his foot on the laminate floor.

Finally Robert opened the door and whisked into the room.

"I'm sorry. I didn't mean to keep you waiting. I had a last minute call from the Feds about Durbin Brown." He sat down, swiveled his chair around, and grabbed the laundry bags. "I think you'll find it's all in there." He handed them to Philip.

Philip clutched the money to his chest. "Who took it?"

"Durbin Brown. He's also wanted for corporate espionage and drug trafficking in three states."

I sat straight up. "Why, that scoundrel. We heard about his underhanded business crimes and watched with the rest of Triville while you arrested him."

Philip leaned toward Robert. "How'd he even know about Mr. Jacobsen's cash?"

"As you've learned, this is a small, gossipy town. He overheard two guys in the drugstore talking about you and Mr. Jacobsen. Apparently, they speculated Mr. Jacobsen would give you cash, and a lot of it. Durbin stayed at the Triville Motel for a couple weeks and figured out who you were. When he saw you with the duffle bags, he put it all together and took a chance the cash was in them."

"How'd you know he had Mr. Jacobsen's money?" Philip asked.

"At first, I didn't. We were watching him because we suspected he was part of a drug deal that went down in Chapsburg. I saw him walking around the motel parking lot with two laundry bags. They were square-shaped, much too symmetrical to have clothes in them. I pulled out my laptop and checked online. Sure enough he'd posted about stealing one million dollars in cash and hiding it in laundry bags."

"You're kidding." Philip emphasized the word kidding.

"No. Criminals are bragging about their capers on the Internet." Robert shook his head. "I cornered Durbin and asked him if he knew anything about any missing money. He turned pale. 'The loot in the laundry bags?' he asked. I knew I had him then. I figured he didn't want any more attention than I'd already given him for fear I'd discover his other crimes. He confessed he'd taken the money from a guy at the motel. I entered his room, and he handed me the stash. While I was in there, I picked up several notes with threatening messages on them that looked as though a child scribbled them." Robert scratched his chin.

I slapped my hand over my mouth. "So that's where they came from. I found some in my shop. They must have been to scare me into shutting down in case his faulty products didn't run me out of business. But how did he place them inside the building without me seeing him?"

Robert thumped his fingers on his desk. "He probably pushed them through the space in the wall after Philip crashed, or he could've squeezed them in between the building and the plastic Pete and Charlie nailed up before they installed the window. I'd guess he did it late at night, or in the wee hours of the morning when you were sleeping. More than likely he parked a ways from the shop and walked to and from the building."

Philip rubbed his hand over the money bags. "How'd he get in my room?"

"As soon as he figured out who you were he waited until the clerk at the front desk left his post.

Then he swooped in the lobby and located a card, plus the code for your room. With his expertise he quickly made a key. All he had to do was look for the money to show up and you to leave it unattended. He brought in the bags of toilet paper and replaced the cash. After I brought him in for theft of the million dollars, some of his big time cronies hired a fancy lawyer who came up here and bailed him out, but Durbin was ordered not to leave town. I gathered enough evidence to make the other charges stick and nailed him."

I scooted up in my seat. "That's when you arrested him, and we all watched."

"Right."

"I'm so dumb for not using the inside bolt on the door."

"You're very bright. You won't make that mistake again," Robert said.

"Huh?"

"Know how I know you're so smart?" Robert placed his palms on the desk.

"No."

I waited for Robert to say something about Philip being a stockbroker and how his company trusted him to get Mr. Jacobsen's account.

"You're dating Eve." Robert shifted his gaze to me and grinned.

I laughed then, and Robert and Philip did too.

Philip shifted the bags on his lap. "I'm concerned about one more thing. Will this be all over the news when Durbin's charged? What about the trial?"

Robert peered at him with kind eyes. "I made a deal with Durbin. Since he gave me the names of several lieutenants and drug dealers in the cartel, I suggested the DA drop the theft charges, especially

since Durbin returned the money. The DA agreed."
Chief Grimes stood.

Joy pierced my heart like an arrow as Philip and I
rose from our seats.

Philip could barely get his palm out and hold onto
the bags, but he managed to shake Robert's hand. "Let
me know if there's anything I can do for you."

"There is. Take good care of Eve."

"My pleasure." Philip's lips turned up.

Robert tilted his head. "And don't go chasing any
more criminals. We arrested Joey and Jack yesterday."
He puffed out his chest and hitched up his belt. "I
assisted the Feds."

Philip stared at Robert. "How'd they get all those
stolen car parts on that isolated mountain?"

"I doubt you could see it when you were there, but
there's a makeshift road going to the warehouse. I
snooped around one day before we arrested them and
had a hard time finding it in broad daylight. It
originates in a washed-out gulley barely noticeable
between the trees and underbrush on either side of it. I
couldn't navigate the deep gap it made in my police
car, but I suspected it was an entrance because of the
width, and it was the only gulch around the area. I
returned to the station and went back in a four-wheel
drive jeep. Once I drove farther up the steep grade, the
roadbed widened."

I touched Robert on the arm. "As good as you are
at what you do, we're lucky you stay in Triville."

Philip straightened. "I don't wonder why you stay
here. I'm moving to Triville. If I ever have any more
trouble I'm coming to you immediately."

Robert gave him a thumbs up.

"I'll see lots of Eve here, but I'm taking her to

hairstylist shows in the Big Apple. Then when she fixes her customers' hair, they'll look like glamorous New York models."

I gave him a light jab on the arm. "Just so you don't run into my shop again."

Thank you

We appreciate you reading this Prism title. For other Christian fiction and clean-and-wholesome stories, please visit our on-line bookstore at www.prismbookgroup.com.

For questions or more information, contact us at customer@pelicanbookgroup.com.

Prism is an imprint of
Pelican Book Group
www.PelicanBookGroup.com

Connect with Us
www.facebook.com/Pelicanbookgroup
www.twitter.com/pelicanbookgrp

To receive news and specials, subscribe to our bulletin
http://pelink.us/bulletin

May God's glory shine through
this inspirational work of fiction.

AMDG

You Can Help!

At Pelican Book Group it is our mission to entertain readers with fiction that uplifts the Gospel. It is our privilege to spend time with you awhile as you read our stories.

We believe you can help us to bring Christ into the lives of people across the globe. And you don't have to open your wallet or even leave your house!

Here are 3 simple things you can do to help us bring illuminating fiction™ to people everywhere.

1) If you enjoyed this book, write a positive review. Post it at online retailers and websites where readers gather. And share your review with us at <u>reviews@pelicanbookgroup.com</u> (this does give us permission to reprint your review in whole or in part.)

2) If you enjoyed this book, recommend it to a friend in person, at a book club or on social media.

3) If you have suggestions on how we can improve or expand our selection, let us know. We value your opinion. Use the contact form on our web site or e-mail us at <u>customer@pelicanbookgroup.com</u>

God Can Help!

Are you in need? The Almighty can do great things for you. Holy is His Name! He has mercy in every generation. He can lift up the lowly and accomplish all things. Reach out today.

Do not fear: I am with you; do not be anxious: I am your God. I will strengthen you, I will help you, I will uphold you with my victorious right hand.
~Isaiah 41:10 (NAB)

We pray daily, and we especially pray for everyone connected to Pelican Book Group—that includes you! If you have a specific need, we welcome the opportunity to pray for you. Share your needs or praise reports at http://pelink.us/pray4us

Free Book Offer

We're looking for booklovers like you to partner with us! Join our team of influencers today and periodically receive free eBooks and exclusive offers.

For more information
Visit http://pelicanbookgroup.com/booklovers